FEAR IN THE MIDDLE OF A VAST FIELD

T0398539

EMERGING VOICES FROM THE MIDDLE EAST

Series editor: *Dena Afrasiabi*

Fear
in the
Middle
of a
vast Field

Cover art & design by Omar Ibrahim
Book design by Allen Griffith of Eye 4 Design

Library of Congress Control Number: 2025933481
ISBN: 9781477331835

The following stories have been previously published: "Smuggling Dostoevsky's Heroes Out of Idlib," "Seven Months with the Witch and Her Groom," and "Cinderella" in *BANIPAL*; "How Kind They Are" in *ArabLit Quarterly*, "My Mother is a Terrorist Gang" in *ArabLit*

FEAR IN THE MIDDLE OF A VAST FIELD

INTRODUCTION

Born in Idlib, Syria to a working-class family in June 1981, Mustafa Taj Aldeen Almosa grew up in a liberal and educated environment of diverse religions, sects and social classes; as a child, teenager, and adult he lived in several cities, something which enriched his life experiences and memories. His father was a well-known short story writer in Syria and across the Arab world. He was also a Communist and member of the Revolution Command Council in Idlib and died in 2012 before the army stormed the city.

Almosa is a graduate of Damascus University's Faculty of Media. He has participated in many short story events in cities within Syria. He has written several articles for a number of Arab and local newspapers. His first literary work, "The Story of Discovery", published in the *Literary Week Newspaper*, was considered a transformative moment in his life, winning first place in the Pioneer Authors' Competition in Syria. In 2003 he won the Arab Writers Union competition in Idlib for his story "I was Born an Orphan", while "A Life in the Fog" won first place in the Green Idlib Contest in its first session. His story "The Snow Sculpture: Night of the Fatal Slap" won the best short story award in Syria's Literary Encounter Festival. In 2011 he came third in the Al-Battani short story competition for his work "People", then went on to win the Sharjah Prize for Arab Creativity in the Arab World in 2012 for his story "A Damp Cellar for Three Painters". Lastly, he won the Dubai Cultural Award for his collection "Seventy-Two Years in a Painting" in 2015, and the ArabLit Short Story Prize for "How Kind They Are" in 2021.

In his writings, Almosa supported the Syrian people's peaceful revolution that demanded freedom and democracy. He did not escape from the attacks the regime carried out in order to muzzle and silence authors, journalists, and artists, especially those that expose the tragedy of Syria and Syrian society. Almosa chose to stay in his home-city Idlib until April 2014, but during that period he was subjected to harassment by the regime; security officers broke into and vandalized his family house several times, and its contents were stolen in an attempt by the regime to retaliate against him and his family.

Almosa lived in hiding for several months, moving from one city to another for fear of arrest, until he heard from friends that his writings, published stories, and articles were putting his life in danger. He was advised to leave Syria as soon as possible for the sake of his safety, and at that time a revolutionary managed to secretly take him out of the city at night and leave him near the Orontes River at the Turkish border in the morning. Almosa managed to arrive in Turkey on the 20th of April 2014 and has lived in several cities since. Almosa explains that he made the decision to leave Istanbul and settle in Reyhanli because of its simplicity as well as its proximity and similarity to his home-city, Idlib. In 2020, Almosa moved to Mardin where he currently studies Sociology at Mardin Artuklu University. These adversities, constant travel, and displacement had a great impact on the writer and informed almost every aspect of his life and, ultimately, his writings.

Almosa is the author of six collections of short stories and four plays that have won him prestigious literary prizes in Syria and across the Arab world. Several of his short stories have been translated into many European languages as well as Turkish, Japanese, Persian, and Kurdish. His fertile imagination has helped him write stories characterized by satire, cynicism, criticism, realism, surrealism, fantasy, and absurdity, and he has succeeded in formulating his own exquisite literary language and style. His work features a compelling formula which combines dark comedy with absurdist fiction to explore important existential questions.

Almosa skilfully deconstructs the world around him to recreate a parallel one inhabited by the narrator—often the writer himself—and other characters. In this dystopian and nightmarish world, Almosa depicts and explores social, political, cultural, religious, ideological, and psychological structures in effect before and during the Syrian war. He adeptly mixes miscellaneous genres in the same text, creating influential and poignant stories which succeed in capturing the feelings as well as the inner psychological metamorphoses experienced by his characters.

The collection includes 28 texts chosen from six collections of short stories published between 2012 and 2020. Although some stories take place in a war-torn country, presumably Syria, others are universal and portray various human subjects, emotions, relationships, and realities. Many of Almosa's stories compel us to experience the harshness of reality, whether set during war or in times of peace, through the portrayal of diverse scenarios: a man befriends a witch and together they fly on her modernized broomstick over checkpoints to besieged territories; a whimsical man believes he is greater than Noah and puts together a plan to save his nation; three conceited painters argue in a bleak cellar which serves as their workshop; a writer is obsessed with the knee of a woman sleeping in front of him on a train on the way to a seaside town; another in search of inspiration decides to isolate himself in a deserted district in order to write; a writer claims to have translated a book from English in the hopes that it will be published, thus exposing cultural and linguistic clashes between East and West. Almosa's characters come from all walks of life. They exist, live, and move in familiar places, by no means exotic, but suddenly the absurd, the supernatural, and the fantastical arise in the guise of a witch, a corpse, a ghost, a genie, or an animal endowed with reason. The daily chilling adversities endured by Syrians since 2011 establishes the tragic disposition of the author, his sense and perception of reality, as much as his taste for absurd and speculative features, in stories of people tormented by the loss of a loved one or forced into displacement and exile, in an eternal search for an alternative homeland and a sense of belonging.

Recurrent themes appear in the stories, such as life, death, and love during war. In some cases, war is depicted literally through descriptions of shelling, bombing, explosions, rubble, and dismembered body parts. But the war is also utilized to bring in fantastical features as a way to portray a parable of love, pain, suffering, displacement, and the never-ending search for belonging. Perhaps this is one of Almosa's techniques to escape adversities and harsh realities: creating a parallel dystopian world. Death and its inevitability is another prevalent theme throughout the collection. Almosa endows his stories with a sense that any moment could be the last, a reality that places the characters and, inevitably, the reader face to face with the brevity and transience of life. This is even more intense because of the war and the struggle to survive.

Fear is also a theme that permeates the stories—the fear of losing a friend, a parent, a loved one, or a homeland. The harrowing feeling of loss unites us as human beings, highlighting the overwhelmingly fleeting nature of our existence and the shared burden of fear and sorrow. This theme is explored in several stories, such as "How Kind They Are", "When One Face Merged into Another" and "Scar in a Modest Poem". Another pervasive fear— the uncertainty of a better future—drives various characters to immerse themselves in existential questions of identity and nationhood, which take center stage in "Half an Hour of Agony", "A Bus Full of Scumbags", "Tale of a Wandering Soul Lost in Europe" and "Smuggling Dostoevsky's Heroes Out of Idlib".

Love features here too. It symbolizes the will to survive, live, and escape the brutality of war. Whenever presented, however, it is often supernatural, unrequited, and marked by strangeness, absurdity, and surrealism—for example, a young waitress who falls in love with a refugee without even knowing his name, or the dead man infatuated with the severed hand of his neighbor's beautiful dead daughter after both of them were massacred, and their dismembered body parts were buried hurriedly and randomly in separate graves. This distorted love often reflects the psychological state of the characters involved, whose lives have been ripped apart and warped either because of the war and its atrocities or because of their innate internal flaws and pressures.

Writing from war-torn Syria, Almosa blurs the line between fiction and reality to draw his readers into the emotional depths of his experiences, expose the complexities of truth, and perhaps shape his own understanding of life, love, imagination, and reality. The often unexpected endings of his stories challenge our judgements as readers. This adds beauty to the stories, broadens the imagination, and involves readers more deeply in the narratives. This collection is a scream against fear and death as much as it is an ode and a homage to life and love in times of both war and peace.

Alice and I set out to translate this collection to increase the visibility of Mustafa Taj Aldeen Almosa and his literary work, which may be less well known in the UK, US, and other English-speaking countries, and bring it to a wider audience, most crucially when these stories relate to lived experiences. We hope that we did justice to these poignant stories, and managed to preserve the exceptional fusion of disparate literary and linguistic techniques.

Maisaa and Alice
Leeds and Edinburgh, February 2025

1 MY MOTHER IS A TERRORIST GANG

Death called me a couple of hours ago and told me in its cold, foggy voice that it wanted to visit me. I accepted and said that I would be here waiting. I was very happy; finally I would get to see Death in person. God! How beautiful this thing was. Of course, I had never seen Death personally—I had only felt it.

I was embarrassed because we did not have any fruit or sweets in the house worthy of such a beautiful guest. We only had tea, coffee, and cough syrup.

Through my happiness I suddenly wondered, "Where did Death get my mobile number?"

I privately guessed that my friend Mazen must have given it.

Mazen had mysteriously disappeared from the streets of Damascus a year ago. I imagined that the naughty Mazen was now in the other world, on a big bus, throwing paper scraps out the window with my number written on them. Death had found one of the scraps on the street and called me.

I used to do this in my adolescence: I threw pieces of paper out the bus window with my home phone number and a paragraph from a song by Hany Shaker, hoping that a beautiful girl would find one and call me, and a love story would begin.

But it never happened. One time, the cleaner called and angrily told my father, "Your number's polluting the streets; it's what's causing the hole in the ozone layer."

"Do you remember, Mazen, when we used to mix gin with cola in the University Faculty of Media cafeteria to drink, get tipsy, and look stealthily at beautiful girls? Do you remember when we went to—"

The bell rang. How punctual in its appointments, our friend Death!

I rushed to the door and opened it. I gasped as I saw Mazen in front of me. We hugged eagerly and laughed. "Oh you devil," I told him. "You really imitate its voice perfectly. Upon my honor, I thought it was Death itself who spoke to me!"

I brought him into my room and we sat down. My mother came in and I introduced her to Mazen.

My mother was an eccentric. Ever since the start of the war, her behavior had been getting increasingly strange with each passing day. As I was introducing her to Mazen she turned her back and walked out, without even greeting him.

I apologized to him and said, "Don't be upset; please forgive me—it's aging and all its ailments."

I went into the kitchen and made two cups of coffee.

On the way back to my room, I passed the living room door. I heard my mother crying as she told our neighbor, "Yesterday, he was talking to Nada and today it's Mazen."

"What's the problem with that?" our neighbor asked, and my mother replied, "The problem is that there's no one in his room, not yesterday and not today. He's talking to his friends who were killed."

The tray dropped from my hands.

Coffee spilled on the tiles.

My mother . . . As always, I had created a dream and let it walk the streets of Damascus, but then she came along . . . and snatched it away.

"My Mother is a Terrorist Gang"
Taken from the collection *Vase from a Massacre*

For ten years, my hair has caused me untold suffering. I always let it grow long, only trimming it very occasionally. It is frizzy but I really wish it was silky soft. Over these years I have tried many creams and oils, but it has remained frizzy. When I walk down the street the lightest gust of wind is enough to make me look like a ghoul. Kids run from me as if I am the snake-haired Medusa herself. Oh, how my long hair has exasperated me and not been what I wanted.

They arrested me yesterday evening. The patrol head greeted me in his own way, and I was very surprised: instead of shaking my hand, he warmly shook my face with his fist, causing one of my teeth to fly from my mouth and land on the street. I read once that certain nations have peculiar habits when it comes to handshakes—kissing noses, for example. I secretly wondered if the patrol head was one of those people. After that, he lovingly kicked me into a car and we went to the security department. I was very upset about my knocked-out tooth; I imagined one of the local kids treading on it, crushing it during a game of football.

At the security department, they affectionately hurled me into a cramped cell. There were dozens of young men in there and I could only just squeeze into the corner. Terrifying shrieks were penetrating our cell from all directions. How lucky those neighbors were: they had televisions to watch the Barcelona vs Real Madrid match and were raucously cheering on the teams.

An hour passed as I looked through a skylight in the roof of the cell, watching the night creep up and the moon scatter feeble light over our bodies. By chance I noticed something written on the wall to my right: *I love you, Lina.* The word 'love' made me sigh. I opened my mouth and grabbed another tooth that was on the verge of falling out. I used it to scratch the following sentence under the first one: *This man loves you, Lina. Damn you! You must understand this fact. Damn you too, Samira, because I love you, but you act like this man's Lina.* Then I drew a heart pierced by a sharp arrow. When I had finished, I put my tooth in my shirt pocket. Oh, what can I say about young women! They never believe that men have equal rights nowadays!

I almost suffocated in the silence of those young men. I turned to my right and gasped when I saw my neighbor.

"Ali Aqla Arsan!"[1] I exclaimed. "You're here? Hello!"

"Hi! But I'm not Ali Aqla Arsan."

Naturally, this was a little trick of my own invention; I often used it on the south route bus to start a conversation with whomever was sitting next to me.

At that moment, the door of the cell opened and the jailer cried out my name. I stood up happily, muttering, "Finally, time for dinner!"

I walked to the door and, before exiting, asked the others, "Want anything from outside?"

Frankly, I was afraid that someone might ask for a kilo of oranges, or a kilo of apples . . . or a Kilo of Michel[2]—the market had actually closed hours ago. No one uttered a word, so I sighed in relief and went away. The jailer kicked my legs, and I fell. He grabbed my right leg, his colleague my left, and they dragged me quickly down a long gloomy corridor. How considerate of them: they did not want me to walk and were protecting my legs from exhaustion. Truly, I felt embarrassed by their kindness.

---

[1] Ali Aqla Arsan is a Syrian politician, writer and president of the Arab Writers Union from 1969 to 2005. His policies conformed to those of the Syrian ruling party and attempted to oppress and silence the voices of free Syrian writers.
[2] Michel Kilo is a Syrian dissident writer and human rights activist.

In the Inspector's room, there was a thin, naked young man on the floor. He was unconscious and covered in blood. The Inspector was taking photos of him on his mobile phone. When he had finished, one of the jailers took the young man out. The Inspector looked at me. I smiled at him. "Why is your hair so long, you asshole?" he shouted at me.

My God: asshole. What a beautiful word, sounding like a sweet melody coming from a piano. It was my uncle's favorite word, what he always called me when we played cards with our friends.

"It's because the barber in our neighborhood is a dissident, so I boycotted him as soon as the cosmic conspiracy against our country started."

"A dissident? Give me his name and address!"

"His name is Taj Aldeen Almosa. He lives in the fourth grave to the right of the olive tree, in the southern graveyard."

The Inspector gave the address to the jailers and ordered them to fetch the so-called Taj immediately. I was over the moon: only the security services would have the ability to reach into the afterworld to bring me back my father, who had passed away a year ago.

The Inspector smiled maliciously as he tied my hands behind my back. Then he gathered my long hair in his hand and tied to it a thick rope. He passed this rope through a metal ring that was hanging from the ceiling. He pulled the rope, assisted by the jailer, and my body rose up. I was dangling from the ceiling by my hair. Wow! I was mesmerized by this amusing notion. I was like a swing. The Inspector started pushing my body toward the jailer and the jailer pushed it back. They were laughing like two little children. I laughed with them; I really liked this game, and I sang them a Fairouz song, *Yara*. But after a few minutes the Inspector yawned and left the room with the jailer to go to sleep for a while, leaving me there alone, hanging from the ceiling by my hair. I was very sad. Why had they not stayed to play with me? What did they have to lose? We had all been enjoying this funny game, the three of us. How kind the Inspector was. But unfortunately, he had forgotten to take my photo with his mobile phone, so I had lost a unique opportunity for fame. I would have had fans, and girls would have chased me wherever I went.

After a few hours blood started to trickle from my forehead over my face. Soon some flies flew up to drink ravenously. After they had finished, one of them came and landed on my nose, smiled at me, and said, "Thank you. Your blood is a true delicacy."

"You're welcome, my friend. I'm happily at your service."

"Can I ask you something?"

"Please do."

"Do you believe in God?"

"Um . . . To be honest, hanging like this, I can't possibly believe in anything."

"You mean you're an atheist."

"I remember being a believer last Tuesday."

We both remained silent for a moment then I exhaled deeply and said, "To be honest, my friend, I don't believe in unreciprocated faith. I believe in faith and counter-faith, and since I was a child, I've felt that God doesn't believe in me."

"Hmm."

Suddenly the Inspector entered the room; the flies panicked and flew off my face. "Goodbye, my love," whispered the one that had spoken to me as it flew away.

The Inspector ordered the jailer to get me down and take me back to the cell. I wanted to ask about dinner, but the jailer kicked my legs again and I fell. He grabbed me by the legs and dragged me back along the gloomy corridor.

From the door of one of the cells along the corridor came the sound of someone screaming. His voice was very similar to my father's. Delighted,

I screamed back, "How are you, Dad? Don't worry about me—the people here are very kind, rest assured. Later, they're going to send us to Addounia TV³ where I'll talk on camera about our important literary experiences. Then we'll take a souvenir photo with the host in the 'Misleading News' section. After that, we'll go home and drink our best *araq*. Don't worry, Dad. Do you have any cigarettes? Just a couple of cigarettes, please, for the sake of the Soviet Union! Please—I'm dying for a cigarette."

Apparently, my father couldn't hear me over the screams of the Barcelona and Real Madrid supporters.

The jailer opened the door to my cell while I lay on the floor. "My father being brought back from the afterworld by the security services will put the *fuqaha* in a very embarrassing position before believers," I thought. "I hope that God will inspire them with the right interpretation."

Then my sweet romantic jailer lifted me up in his arms as if I was his beloved and threw me gently into the cell.

Under the faint light of the moon penetrating the room through the skylight, I tried to look for Ali Aqla Arsan, but one of the men tapped me on the shoulder and whispered, "Do you know anything about corpses?"

"Yes, I do—most of my family died in my arms."

"Please, can you check if this guy's dead or not? I can't see well enough."

I looked where he was pointing and saw the thin naked man from before. I leaned over him and took his head between my hands, lifting it toward the moonlight. I moved my face toward his until our noses touched. I stared deeply into his eyes and saw my face clearly reflected in them . . . I gasped sharply. My frizzy hair was silky soft; I couldn't believe it. I let the young man's head fall to the floor and caressed my hair. Only then was I certain that it really had become as soft as silk.

---

³ A Syrian pro-regime television channel known for disseminating government propaganda and sanctioned by the EU in 2011 for inciting violence.

My mind soared with happiness. I stood in the middle of the cell laughing madly. I clapped my hands and swayed joyfully. Everyone applauded me, including Lina and Samira from the wall. They cheered my primitive dance. I danced for a long time beside the corpse of the thin young man. I danced ecstatically like a drunk jester and through the small skylight in the roof, the moon wept some more light upon us from above.

14th July, 2013
"How Kind They Are!"
Taken from the collection *Half an Hour of Agony*

I remember that the car which extinguished my friend's life was the same one that transported what remained of mine to this place.

All of us ill and injured walked along the narrow corridors like ghosts, leaning sometimes against the walls, sometimes on the drip stands.

An old man passed between us pushing his metal food trolley, but none of us took our share of the poorly cooked offerings.

At the same time, the angel of death snoozed in the corner, getting some rest before returning to sweep us up like human residue.

On every bed lay a patient, each reflecting on scenes from the film of their life. The clips would come randomly, as if made by an amateur. It was only the cancer patient who, after a third dose of chemotherapy, could edit the scenes in his head like a professional filmmaker.

The nurse on duty, who did not like cinema, indifferently distributed medication to the patients sometime before midnight, then went to his room to caress behind its door the breasts of his female counterpart.

One day, the wife of this nurse and the husband of the other would end up in this hospital themselves; human scraps lying on the rickety beds, producing in their own imaginations films of love they had never lived.

The angel of death sat beside me on my bed, and I lit a cigarette for him. He took a quiet drag, and I slowly blew its smoke out through my nostrils. Karl Marx would call this the 'division of labor', I thought, but God knows best.

The patient on my right had a long rosary and was counting out the 99 Names of God on its beads. The names of Allah would end but his pain would not.

I went to the bathroom to drink a bottle of cheap wine, hoping to numb my own pain. Then I staggered back, swiping the rosary from the unmoving hand of my neighbor, who had just died.

On my bed under the threadbare blanket, I started counting the beads, babbling to myself. The 99 Pains of God would end but my names would not.

The hospital toilets were a hideous nightmare for the patients. Whenever they passed by the small mirrors over the washbasins, it was not themselves they saw.

One evening in a frenzy I drew a face resembling mine on each of these mirrors with a lipstick I had taken from an old sweetheart as a memento.

No one ever smiled here: not the patients or their visitors, not the doctors or the nurses or the old cook, not I or the angel of death, not even the drip stand.

It was only Mr. President, inside his huge portrait hanging in the lobby, who did.

"How much does a kilo of smiles cost today, Boss?" I screamed at him, enraged, making everyone around me jump in fright.

He did not answer and the people in the lobby moved away from me with soft gasps.

I left this place on crutches, I and the rest of my names; we returned to our neighborhood and for the next year and a half watched the street demonstrations from the balcony, then the missiles destroying the houses.

At night, I practiced my hobby of writing little short stories about the war, the dead, the military and my pains, and the neighbors' beautiful daughter.

This is word-for-word what happened to me . . . and then arrived the two angels to test my faith.

Just as I had been imagining every night since leaving the hospital, now the soldiers flocked to massacre us completely.

Last night, they raided our neighborhood and quickly rounded us up in the square. We were few since most of the local families had been displaced a long time ago.

After they had us gathered, they started slaughtering us with their knives and machetes, roaring with laughter.

"Little short stories?" a soldier screamed in my face. "By God, I'll chop you into tiny little pieces!"

Then he felled me with his axe.

They made sure we were dead, wiped our blood off their hands in disgust, then got into their cars and sped off, leaving behind our bodies and limbs.

After they were certain the soldiers had gone, residents of the bordering neighborhood quietly snuck into ours. They collected our corpses and body parts and then dug modest graves to bury us haphazardly in the darkness of the night.

Of course, we were very grateful, and it was very tiring for them. Unfortunately, though, due to the lack of good acquaintanceship between us, as well as a dearth of tools, many mistakes and comical cockups occurred during the burials.

Some body parts were buried with the wrong corpse, so that the mish of limbs became mixed up with the mash of bodies.

Thus, in each grave were the remains of more than one person; each corpse was a mismatched outfit assembled by someone who did not understand the art of style.

So after I was buried, for example, I turned to my severed hand and gasped: it was not mine. I knew my own hand very well (we went way back).

However, I was soon rejoicing when I realized I had the hand of our neighbors' daughter, the girl who had been captivating all the guys with her beauty for years. She and her family had been slain with us.

My happiness was such that it overflowed my grave, for I had long dreamed of this beautiful woman and her delicate hands.

I breathed the hand in with joy then felt slightly dizzy; it seemed that the final thing she had done in life was to put on perfume.

I kissed it gently—how soft it was. I kissed it many more times, imagining that my own hand was now in her grave, and she was resting her face upon it, just like she used to do on her balcony when we were alive.

As my eternity began I was half drunk, engrossed in lovingly kissing her hand.

My gentle kisses, nothing else, were my only answers to the angels' repeated questions.

22nd March, 2014
"My Names Between the Hospital and Eternity"
Taken from the collection *The Last Friend of a Beautiful Woman*

My grandfather buried my umbilical cord and planted a tree over it. From that time on, I no longer knew who I was: was I me or Yahya or the loquat tree? The shell that just landed on me persuaded me that my years of life would not exceed the number of the tree's branches.

Once, in the capital, I fell and injured my hand. My mother suddenly awoke, frightened, in her villa in the north; she went out onto the balcony and looked down at the loquat tree. Hurriedly fetching a ladder, she ascended courageously to a branch that had been broken by the wind. She bandaged it slowly. In the morning my hand was healed.

"You won't survive long after my departure," Yahya said confidently. "Goodbye, Yaman." He leaned forward to kiss me gently on the lips, like we were any two lovers. He carried a bag in which he had collected all of my paintings without their frames. He waved and left. This had happened this morning after a strange night when Yaman and I had reconciled for the first time in three decades, a few hours before the missile landed on me in the street by the big garden.

I was bleeding heavily. Blood: that strange color in which—after Yahya, stoned, had embedded my knife in my shoulder—I had drunkenly painted my most beautiful painting. The color of blood is the only original one among all the colors of life.

With difficulty, I managed to drag myself away from among the dead and wounded. I walked the few streets to our old abandoned villa.

I had refused any help; convinced I was going to die, the only first aid I required was to return to our deserted home to do so. The place I had been born. Of course, there was a massive difference: I had been born amidst luxurious furniture and highly elegant people, and while I would now die here too, it would be among clutter and ghostly memories of a bizarre life, the remains of objects, their dust, along with a brief summary of my life like a faded motion picture, passing through my memory like a train sounding a dreary whistle.

I did not think I would have more than half an hour to remember all of my life, my strange life. But I would try as I lay here, dying.

I do not know where my father came from although it was said that he was from an impoverished and distant village obsessed with superstitions. The people of his village exiled him when he was a teenager due to his frequent attacks on the shrines, sanctuaries, and holy places there.

The old Turkish woman told me a great deal about those days: how my mother fell in love with my father and forced my grandfather to accept her marriage to one of the children of the peasants he so hated. On a warm evening, the old woman told me another of her stories.

"Your grandfather wept the day you were born. You weren't crying like any other newborn—you came out of your mother silent; it was astonishing. We couldn't find a convincing explanation for it. You got your mother's blue eyes and her white complexion—your face was an evolution of her stunning beauty. You were like a light that made us gasp, that would make whoever else saw you gasp too. Your grandfather couldn't believe it. He hugged you to his chest and cried, he who hadn't cried his entire life. He described you as 'the shepherd of the women'. Your grandfather grew up surrounded by women: his mother, then his stepmother, several aunts on both sides and his sisters; he had no uncles or brothers. He married your grandmother who gave birth to your aunt and your mother. Your aunt gave birth to Rima and your mother gave birth to Samaher and Yusra, then you—thus breaking the circle of women around your grandfather.

"It was he who let your blond hair grow and fall around your shoulders like silk. He combed it for you every evening at his table on the balcony, as if he wanted all the people in his life to see you.

"Your father wasn't home on the day you were born. As usual, he was with his friends planning and explaining the war that would restore justice to the entire planet."

Oh, old Turkish woman! My father's war came after his death. It was too late, and it only killed his son.

The Turkish woman knew all the stories of our home. As a child, she had become lost when the Sanjak of Alexandretta was annexed to Turkey. She walked for several nights until she arrived here. My grandfather was young. He convinced his family to take in this little Turkish girl, and she spent her life in a small room behind our villa, serving the family and dreaming of returning to Turkey one day.

The first painting I did, in the cellar of canvases where my father used to go to paint away from my mother and grandfather, was of the old Turkish woman's face. That night I ran to her room to give her my first painting, only to discover her dead in her bed, her dream of returning to Turkey a second corpse beside her.

When I was born, they saw me and called me Yaman. They did not see him, so he lived for five years without a name. When I noticed him, I named him Yahya. For nearly three decades, Yahya was my terrible secret.

The quarrels between my mother and father continued for a decade. When he could no longer bear her arrogance and vanity, he deserted us. He left the cellar of canvases for me to learn to paint and went to live far away from us. No one was able to bring him back until cancer succeeded in doing so two decades later, just a few weeks before his death.

During the day, in front of other people, my mom was haughty, but at night she cried silently in her bed.

In the cellar of paintings, I did not depict the poor or the peasants as my father had done. I painted the beautiful women whom I had loved throughout my life from childhood to university.

Behind every painting there was a sweetheart, and behind every sweetheart, a disappointment, and this disappointment was a collection of colors crying on the canvas. I would have to remember them all, now, before I died.

I painted them in a trance of exotic colors, of wine, sorrow, lust, and a lover's smile. When I painted a woman, I started with a breast and finished with her smile.

Only Nadia would I fail to depict. "Nobody can paint Nadia", screamed the demons in my soul, while Yahya chuckled at her naked body in the cellar of paintings.

That night before she left, after she had put on her clothes, she told me, "I might not come back to you. I want you to remain a dream. There's a beautiful loquat tree in the corner of your garden—hang a swing on one of its branches and wait for me. I might return one day."

Damn her dazzling femininity! In front of all my other paramours I would cross my legs and paint them nonchalantly. But with her—what can I say! My soul prostrated itself reverently in front of her naked body and all of my tubes of paint abandoned their bleeding.

Among all of our artist friends, Nadia alone would succeed in painting me.

"Your face is hard to draw, my friend," said Muataz. "It looks like wine. It can be drunk but not drawn."

"Your face is a new color in its own right," muttered Rita.

"Perhaps after a thousand paintings and lovers, I might be able to paint you," Samar whispered.

"You!" Sami shouted after several unsuccessful attempts at his studio in one of the old neighborhoods of the capital. He broke his brush angrily. "Nobody can paint you except God."

But Nadia did.

Completely unlike my painting style, she started with my smile and finished with my blue eyes.

There were a few hours between the third dose of chemo and my father's death. It seemed to us that he had become young again. He said he wanted to paint, and we thought he was longing for his peasants and the village. "I'll paint Yaman," he told us. He smiled and I was happy.

He sat behind the easel and painted for a few hours. He worked with a great euphoria, as if he were making love to my mother their first night together—the first and last night of love between impoverished peasants who were as angry as a raging storm and the noble rich with all their elegance. He had told me about it once, drunk and sorrowful, as he smoked a couple of cigarettes.

He grew tired so he went back to his bed and lay down.

I looked at his unfinished painting and gasped. This face was not mine but Yahya's. At that moment, I realized that my father knew my terrible long-kept secret.

I smiled at him. He smiled back then died.

I wept, embracing him. In the cellar, the beautiful women in my paintings, the peasants in his—even the old Turkish woman in her grave— all of them wept.

Yahya alone leaped around like a lunatic, taking commemorative pictures of us with the corpse.

For a decade my mother had tried to bring God into our home; she felt that God was her last weapon to defeat my father, but my father had always tried to leave God outside.

There was a great misunderstanding between God and my father. I think I inherited this misunderstanding from him, and this war had made me especially aware of it. Throughout my childhood I had imagined God as an old man standing in front of our villa, one foot inside the door, the other still outside.

That night I saw him for the first time—not God, but Yahya.

It was past midnight when I crept into the cellar with the curiosity of a child missing his father. He was asleep; his fingers were stained with paint and his breath smelt of wine. I wandered among his paintings of the peasants. I found half a bottle of wine, drank it and staggered upstairs. In the darkness of the lounge, faint moonlight coming through the window, my mother saw me. Her shadow was as lofty as her personality, with all her majesty.

I walked to the door and opened it. I put my right foot outside and kept the left inside.

"Go back to bed!" my mother shouted at me with her usual obstinacy.

My chronic fear of her prevented me from replying. My life would end but my fear of her would be endless. "I will not," Yahya said to her.

It was then that I saw him for the first time, and after that we would never leave each other. Also, at that moment, for the first and last time, my mother slapped me.

I am sorry for inheriting my father's paints while rejecting the cigarettes rolled hastily by his simple people in favor of the luxury cigars of my mother's magnificence. My father's death crippled her, but her splendor remained intact.

My 'half hour' has passed, everything is over. Who is painting my body?

As I close my eyes, I notice through the broken glass of the lounge window the faded loquat tree in my grandfather's garden, bending over the wall of this big and deserted house, to paint something upon it with its branches.

29th December, 2014
"Half an Hour of Agony"
Taken from the collection *Half an Hour of Agony*

Some shells fell on the main street of the market. After a few moments, the child got up from among the dead and wounded. He was in pain.

He noticed that his hand was missing; he started looking for it among the chaos of the dismembered human body parts.

Suddenly he spotted another severed hand which looked as if it belonged to the body of an old man.

The child picked it up and put it on his wrist, foolishly examining it for a few seconds.

Then he started jumping happily among the corpses and around the wounded, shouting loudly, 'I've grown up! I've grown up! I've grown up!'

"The Child and the War"
Taken from the collection *Vase from a Massacre*

Hastily and under the cover of night, only her eyes showing above a scarf covering her face, Cinderella was pasting opposition posters on the wall of an old alley.

From a distance, the king's soldiers saw her. They chased her through the alleys, but she disappeared. All they found was one of her shoes.

News of this reached the king and he was furious. He ordered his army to go to all the cities in the kingdom, force people to try on the shoe and kill anyone whose foot it fitted.

Over the course of a few months, the soldiers stormed all the cities, towns and villages, leaving huge massacres in their wake, because the feet of everyone—men and women, children and elders—fitted the shoe.

When all the people were terminated, the soldiers returned to their king, who awarded them victory medals and insignia.

Despite this, Cinderella has continued to show up every few nights in the alley to put opposition posters up on the wall.

Then she runs away, leaving her shoe behind every time.

"Cinderella"
Taken from the collection *Vase from a Massacre*

Outraged, he silently cursed the god of boredom with terrible words. He was here on his own, like a ghost with blurred features, exiled from any kind of talk. The harsh silence entertained itself by desecrating his mood throughout the long hours. He exhaled and spat on the tiles, only for half of his saliva to dribble onto his dull khaki uniform.

It was now late afternoon. He had been standing foolishly in this corner like a statue carved from anger since early morning; here, behind a barricade of sandbags on a high roof overlooking the square.

Bored, he looked down at the square every couple of minutes through his rifle's scope, hoping that fate would send him a person to kill with a single bullet. This would render his presence meaningful and slightly quiet the cackling of his boredom.

But no one dared to cross the square. News had spread through the town that there was a dark specter from the military on the roof of the town hall whose hobby was hunting those crossing the plaza. Unfortunately for him, the cats also seemed to be aware of his presence here, for they had stopped crossing the square too. He had initially intended to kill one of them to amuse himself.

His limbs were almost frozen on this grim February day, one of the countless monotonous days to pass during this long war.

He crouched between the sandbags which were like his little fortress. Nostalgia for his distant village drew images in his memory. He wished that he could take a few days off to return to his mother and her delicious food.

A faint voice disturbed the silence around him. He stood up again behind his rifle and scanned the square through its scope. Then he caught sight of an elderly man walking slowly along with a cane.

"Time for work," he said with a malicious smile, aiming at the old man's head. He fired a single shot, and the man fell to the ground, hot blood gushing from his head.

The yellow smile on the sniper's face widened until it had devoured most of his hazy features; relief tinged with a soft joy crept into his mood, rescuing him from the boredom of the past several hours.

He pranced asininely to a second corner of the roof, urinated, then returned to his rifle. Through the scope he was surprised to see two scared-looking young men beside the old man, trying to pull his body away quickly.

Laughing, he fired two bullets. His rifle laughed along with him; it had not worked for some time, to the point that it had almost forgotten the mission for which it had been created. The two new bodies piled up on top of the first one in a random way befitting this chaotic death. Killing these three made him happy; there was now a clear purpose for his presence here.

He lit a cigarette happily and took a drag. Then he looked down at the square and the streets that ran into it like streams. He scanned the old buildings that overlooked the area. Nothing but silence could be heard.

For a while, he imagined that he was a king in the Middle Ages and that this square with its abandoned buildings was his magnificent kingdom. He stretched out his arms and closed his eyes. He raised his face to breathe in the cold air. He was in a euphoric trance that shook his being, revived all the cells of his body and—

Something wet dropped on his forehead. He wiped it with his fingers and discovered that a bird had shat on him. His curses rose into the air and the euphoria evaporated from his soul as though it had never been there. Burning anger erupted on his features and he reached for his rifle. He started to search for the bird through the scope, intent on giving it a bullet for its shit. Outraged, he hunted for it for several minutes but could not find it. He cursed all birds, his insults rolling along behind one another like a pack of black linguistic beasts.

He then caught sight of the creature as it landed on the shoulder of the last corpse. He bit his lower lip slyly, aimed his rifle and fired. To his surprise, the bullet hit the corpse's shoulder, lodging itself in the flesh, two fingers away from the bird. Even more surprisingly, the bird did not seem to be at all bothered by the bullet. It was hopping indifferently around on the back of the body like nothing had happened, as if out for a romantic stroll.

By now he was enraged and determined to turn the bird into the fourth corpse. He aimed his rifle again and fired, but this time he hit the body in its back.

He could not believe what was happening; he was one of the most skilled soldiers in his battalion for the accuracy of his aim—he could even hit a needle from a distance—but his famed talent was now betraying him.

He snarled like a monster. He felt that this bird was his greatest-ever nemesis, that it was mocking him and his skill as a sniper.

For a third time, he aimed his rifle at the bird. By this time, it had hopped over to the corpse's head. He let loose yet another bullet along with an obscene insult.

However, neither of these hit the bird. The bullet penetrated the head of the corpse, leaving its death undisturbed, while the insult was lost in the cold air.

Then, as if the window of opportunity it had given the sniper to kill it had timed out, the bird flew off, soaring high and disappearing beyond the horizon.

He searched for it for a long time, wishing to crush it under his boot for mocking him, but to no avail.

As he cursed the bird which had so offended him, the night slowly loosened its hangings over the sides of the square and a fine drizzle fell slowly in the cold February breeze.

He shivered and lit a cigarette, then grabbed from among the sandbags a bottle of wine that his colleague had given him that morning at the start of his shift.

He had never been a drinker of wine before, but his colleague had recommended it as the best medicine against a disease called cold. He opened the bottle and drank from it thirstily as he smoked his cigarette. He squeezed himself between the sandbags like a child to protect his body from the evening rain.

He liked the taste of wine. He grinned, revealing his decaying teeth, then drank again from the bottle.

As he listened to the monotonous rhythm of the rain, he imagined himself chewing the bird mercilessly between his molars after he had roasted it alive on a fire.

He drank the rest of the wine then lit another cigarette. The whistling and howling of the cold wind between the silent buildings kept him from falling asleep.

The next hour passed without his noticing as he meditated upon the raindrops hitting the pavement. Beautiful images of his distant village passed through his memory, and he sighed.

He groaned as, in solitude, he watched the night sky closely; there was no moon in its dome nor any star on its dark body. A mild dizziness started to play around his head.

He wanted to drink more wine but saw that there was nothing left in the bottle. A fit of laughter seized him suddenly. He laughed until his eyes were watering. He had no idea why or where all the laughter had come from, but he laughed like a madman until he was almost suffocating, the noise echoing across the square.

He lit another cigarette and unbuttoned the jacket of his uniform. His body temperature had increased; sweat broke out on his forehead.

He remembered the three corpses and got up heavily to salute them as the clock struck midnight in the rain. Nothing new had happened to them except that they were now drenched in rainwater so that their blood flowed in a short thin stream into the earth around a huge decades-old tree a couple of meters from the mess of their arbitrary deaths.

He thought he saw something moving close by . . . He could just make out a woman in black emerging from a nearby alley in the darkness. She crossed the square silently in the rain, approaching the bodies.

He made up his mind to shoot her, but when he looked at her through the scope of his rifle, he gasped in shock. His limbs shook and his heart sank. He could not believe what he was seeing—the woman in black was his mother.

He raised his head from his rifle, standing up to look down at her. He stammered and mumbled unintelligibly.

He shouted to her in the silence of the night, but she did not pay him the slightest attention, as if she had not heard his voice. He could see in her eyes an enormous hatred for him. He stood there with a lump in his throat, almost choking, as he observed a tear on his mother's cheek.

She bent down over the corpses, embracing the first one as if it were her baby. She lifted up the body and gently slung it over her shoulder, then turned to return to the alley from which she had appeared.

He called to her, waving at her like a lunatic, but she did not look at him. It seemed as if he did not exist to her, was nothing but an old memory lost in the crowd of her other recollections, as if he were not even her son.

He grew tired of shouting and fell silent. However, when he saw her coming back, he started yelling again and pleading loudly, but she leaned over the second corpse and picked it up, indifferent to his shouts and pleas to look at him.

Heavy tears mixed with raindrops on his face. He felt that his mother no longer wanted him to be her son and instead intended to become a mother to those bodies. The dizziness in his head gnawed like a hungry dog at the cells in his brain.

He rushed to stand next to the wall of the roof, leaning forward as his mother returned to carry the third body away, still resolutely not looking at him, even as his screams and pleas drew other people around. She was acting as if she had never known him, as if he was just a dog barking at the edge of the road. He begged her hysterically and with horrific pain that tore at his soul to look at him, but she picked up the third corpse and again turned around to walk quietly into the alley.

As she slowly moved away, the echo of his pleas shattered his soul, bruising it even further. His spirit was crushed under the weight of his mother's apathy toward him. As she disappeared into the alleyway for the last time, he rushed to jump from the roof, intending to follow her, to kneel down at her feet and pray for her to forgive him and—

His body fell from the top of the building. It hit the pavement and his blood splattered randomly around.

The cold surrounded his corpse, which lay like a crumpled rag in the rain and darkness of the night. Together, the rainwater and his heavy blood formed a short, narrow stream which ran into the mouth of a nearby sewer.

No one but the cold noticed his body lying there on the pavement, like a ghost with blurred features, a few meters from three other bodies heaped one on top of the other in a long, warm embrace.

It was only the bird that came back. It saw the sniper's corpse and landed atop it, hopping quietly around as if on a romantic stroll.

16th March, 2012

"The Sniper"

Taken from the collection *Half an Hour of Agony*

The notebooks scattered like elegant corpses on my table had depressing, empty souls. I had bought them in the various cities I visited throughout the year, hoping to write my novel on their pages. However, due to my mood which felt dark and mysterious, I had failed to begin. A few weeks after I arrived in this city, I felt disgusted by it. It looked to me like a veiled woman. I could not live here with the cold, and I decided to leave so that the cold could enjoy her veil alone. I booked a place on the midnight train to a distant, warm, and beautiful town by a fascinating sea. It was said that it was a town garbed in a short dress; surely it would be suitable for writing a novel. The train would arrive there at dawn after passing through the stations of several cities.

I packed my meager things—a few books and notebooks, some simple clothes, and several pens. My large bag had always provoked laughter from the inspectors at the stations during my non-stop travels throughout the year: why this big bag for these few things? I personally had no answer, which is why I always left to their simple imaginations the freedom to find one.

It was a cold night at the station, and I smoked as I waited for the train. A few travelers were scattered around me here and there. The train arrived with a somber whistle. I looked at my ticket then boarded the specified carriage.

I was walking indifferently between the seats when I caught sight of a beautiful woman and gasped. She was in a deep sleep on two adjacent seats and her dress had ridden up a little, revealing her delectable knees. I hurried forward, intending to sit opposite her.

Suddenly, beside her two seats, I bumped into a man who had appeared from the other direction. He must be her husband. I felt embarrassed. Still, he invited me to sit down in a nervous voice. We sat next to each other in front of her, no one but us in this carriage.

I began to steal glances at her knees without drawing her husband's attention. How beautiful this sleeping woman was.

We passed through several stations. The rain was pouring down heavily in the night of these successive cities and villages. If she were my wife, I would write a novel on her body every night, from her shoulders to these lovely knees. How lucky this buffoon was; if he would only get lost for a minute so I could touch her knee with my fingertips. Although I had run my hands over many women's bodies, I had never before felt such a desire as I did to touch her marble knee; a wild, insatiable desire that was indifferent to the dreary sounds of the rain, the train's whistle, the squealing of the wheels on the track, or to the face of this fool.

Whenever the train entered a tunnel the carriage would sink into darkness, so I decided that in the next tunnel, I would lean forward and stealthily touch her knee without her husband noticing. Before I reached this decision, we had gone through several tunnels; afterward, there were no more. Damn the tunnels: when I needed them, they disappeared.

I yearned to smoke. I excused myself from her husband and exited the carriage onto the gangway. As I lit a cigarette the train entered a tunnel, and I cursed my luck. When it emerged into the light, I started to see her husband's face in front of me with its stupid smile. He asked me for a cigarette; I handed him one and we smoked silently together. My cigarette was finished before his, so I hastened back to touch her knee before he could finish, but the son of a bitch immediately followed me. I exhaled furiously and we sat down together in front of her.

The train moved along the coast, but I was not watching the sunrise or the seagulls in the distance. I was watching the reflection of her sleeping body and her knees in the window. How sweet she was.

The train arrived at the seaside town. I got up, saying goodbye to her beauty with one final look. I took my bag and walked away. She would wake up now and never know that there had been a strange man sitting in front of her for hours through the many stations during the night, that he loved her so much and—

Fingers tapped me on the shoulder from behind. I turned around and it was him. "Sir, you forgot to wake your wife up," he exclaimed. "This is the final stop."

"*My* wife? I thought she was *your* wife!"

We gasped and my heart dropped with his, crashing onto the floor of the carriage. We ran back to her like two lunatics, stumbling over each other.

Humans normally wake up other humans by shaking them by the shoulder, but not me and this man. Unconsciously, I put my hand on one of her knees and he his hand on the other; we shook her vigorously.

She toppled from the seat and fell, her body lifeless. We bent over in horror to see death on the features of her face. The silence of death hung in the carriage, disturbed only by the distant sounds of seagulls and waves.

We did not know anything about her. We did not know her name, at which station she had boarded the train, nor at which station she had died. What we did know was that two moronic strangers had sat through several stations during a rainy night staring lustfully at the knees of a dead woman. Her death made us forget our desire and awakened a great sadness inside us. It was like a violinist creeping inside us to play desolate music.

We were a little confused about what to do with her corpse. I emptied my large bag of my meager belongings and we crammed her body into it.

We heaved the bag onto the seat then divided up her things between us and also took a shoe each for remembrance. We disembarked the train with sad faces, leaving behind my bag, her coffin, and hoping that the train would take her back to her city.

Within a couple of days, I had arranged a room overlooking the sea. That evening, I sat at my table by the window, pondering the waves and gulls as I smoked and drank half a bottle of wine.

I ignored all the notebooks I had accumulated from those various cities to instead start enthusiastically writing my novel in this other humble one—page one, two, three, and so on.

I loved this notebook very much, although it was not I who had bought it. I had found it two nights ago, there in the railway carriage, where that beautiful woman had placed it on her seat as a cushion for her quiet death.

1st March, 2015
"Sleeping Beauty in a Railway Carriage"
Taken from the collection *Fear in the Middle of a Vast Field*

9   VASE FROM A MASSACRE

The shells fell heavy as rain on the village square where a modest wedding was in progress.

The terrified father ran to the square to look for his wife. Their young son followed him.

The father could not find the mother among the bodies since the facial features of some of the corpses had melted.

One of the wounded reassured him that he had seen her leaving the party a few minutes before the shells fell.

The child was having fun, happily picking up dismembered human hands, thinking them to be toys. He had collected several hands before his father shouted at him, ordering him to go home immediately, and promising that he would return home soon with his mother.

The child ran home clutching the hands to his chest.

Once in the living room, he picked up a vase from the table, removed the flowers and replaced them with the hands. He placed the vase beside him on the couch, smiling mindlessly.

His father and mother were late, and the child yawned and soon dozed off beside the vase.

When he had fallen asleep, one of the hands silently reached toward him from the vase and tenderly stroked his soft hair.

"Vase from a Massacre"
Taken from the collection *Vase from a Massacre*

For two winters, it did not leave her dreams. For two winters, she deprived herself of everything to save up for it.

For two winters, she saw it on her shoulders in her rose-colored dreams.

Now she had all the money she needed in her possession. She invited her friends to share in this momentous life event, and they rushed to the largest display of coats in the city where she bought a very luxurious fur coat.

She cried happily in the car on the way back while her friends ululated.

At home, surrounded by the absolute silence of her friends, she approached the tall mirror, holding her breath, and put on the fur coat.

A storm of admiring applause from her friends swept the room, echoing along with their gasps.

She secretly wished for a second that the three other seasons would die, that only winter would stay alive, so that this fur could remain on her shoulders forever.

She stroked her coat for several minutes, as if it were her lover, contemplating it lovingly in the mirror. Its beauty enchanted her, and her soul was intoxicated.

She did not notice, however, that she herself was not visible in the mirror.

It was only the fur coat that appeared there.

24th April, 2014
"The Coat"
Taken from the collection *Fear in the Middle of a Vast Field*

On a dark and moonless night, men in dark clothing besieged an ancient palace and arrested an old violin, long famed for its sweet music.

They dragged it by the strings like a dog to one of their cellars and tortured it brutally for several days until it confessed to everything they had taught it.

Next morning, the interrogator told his master proudly that the process of educating the violin had been successful, but the master did not believe him.

The interrogator smiled nastily and called the darkly dressed men. They brought the violin out of the cellar and threw it on a chair in front of the master's desk.

Keen to make his master believe him, the interrogator looked at the pale violin and motioned at it to begin, whereupon the violin, sad and defeated, began to play the anthem of the country's ruling party.

"The Violin"
Taken from the collection *Vase from a Massacre*

I don't know them; I've never met any of them. They say they know me! Oh my God, they're crazy.

Seven months ago, I was standing at our front door, smoking. I sighed as I thought about the city market I missed so much. I hadn't been able to go for a year because of the damned military checkpoint at the entrance to our neighborhood.

Suddenly, a witch landed beside me on her broomstick.

"I'll take you to the market," she said. "Come—get on."

I sat behind her on the broom. It was not made of straw, like the brooms you read about in old fairy tales; this one was a vacuum cleaner!

I asked her why and she explained: "It's the need for modernity in fairy tales. The technological development in those stories has foisted it upon me. Your cigarette's bothering me, by the way."

I threw my cigarette away and a passing bird caught it and continued smoking. We flew higher, passing over the military checkpoints. When we landed at the market, I ran joyfully amongst the people. I hugged the vegetable carts and kissed Haj Kasem, the cake vendor.

A couple of hours later I returned to the witch at the entrance to the market. She switched on her vacuum cleaner, and I rode behind her back to the house.

In this way, every day for seven months, the witch took me to market then brought me back to the house, free of charge. Each time we passed over the checkpoints, we spat on the soldiers and laughed.

During one flight I surreptitiously urinated on the soldiers below. One of them raised his head happily.

"If Mr. President hadn't prayed for rain yesterday, it wouldn't be raining!" he shouted.

During another flight, when we were in the middle of the sky, I whispered to the witch, "There's a women-only swimming pool in the north of the city. Men aren't allowed. What do you think of flying over it, just quickly?"

"Oh, that's very disrespectful!" she shouted angrily at me over her shoulder.

"I only meant to fly above it in an innocent, respectful way," I replied. "Just to look, not with any bad intentions. It's not like I want to drop barrel bombs on them!"

"You must have been brought up very badly! And—"

But at that moment we swerved to avoid hitting a cloud. The witch was flying her vacuum with amazing proficiency.

The very last time we flew on the vacuum cleaner, it stopped working in midair.

"The battery's dead!" the witch screamed as we began to fall. "I forgot to charge it last night!"

I smashed into the ground and was knocked out cold. A day, a week, a month—I don't know how long, but while unconscious I had horrifying nightmares: thin bodies, immense fear, stifled, rattling breaths, insane torture, dismembered body parts, cries of pain, coagulated blood, electric currents being passed through bodies, satanic cackles, crushed skulls, broken bones, mortal demons toying with human beings in dark cellars, a tongue-like piece of meat dumped on the ground, rotten bodies, darkness and overcrowding and—

I came round slowly, my body in great pain. I realized I was lying on a sofa surrounded by people I didn't know. They said they were my friends and family—a pale woman said she was my mother. She was explaining to them that I had been arrested seven months ago by our doorstep, on charges of participating in demonstrations. She explained how I was so brutally tortured that I lost my memory.

Beside her stood a foolish-looking teenager who said he was my brother. He proclaimed proudly in front of them all that my slogans and cheering had been the most magnificent in all of the demonstrations.

My God! Where had they got all this bizarre stuff from? I tried to talk but couldn't: someone had stolen my tongue!

After everyone had gone, the pale woman covered me up and went with the teenager into another room, leaving me alone in the darkness with my suffering.

A few hours later, the witch approached the sofa. She was bathed in a bright light. She bent over to place her hand tenderly on my hair; her whiteness had increased since the last time I saw her.

"We're going to go on a final, wonderful journey now," she whispered to me.

When she lifted me up, all of my pain disappeared, as though it had never existed at all.

She walked to the porch, put me on the vacuum, got on in front of me and switched it on.

And off we flew, quietly, higher and higher—higher than all the previous times, to the edge of the heavens.

"Why don't you teach me how to drive this thing?" I suggested to her.

She turned to me, smiling gently. "It'll be my pleasure," she said. "When we get to the other world, I'll teach you how to drive the vacuum cleaner."

"Is there a swimming pool for women in the other world that we can fly over?" I asked

"Yes, there is," she replied. "And we can—"

But *oops!* We had to swerve to avoid that cloud again.

21st February, 2014
"Seven Months with the Witch and her Broom"
Taken from the Collection *The Last Friend of a Beautiful Woman*

If his coat had a memory, it would be crowded with images of the bodies that had passed through it over the decades. Many different bodies, indeed, but they all had the same smell—the smell of ordinary people. His coat resembled an old man who was only one step away from the grave. Despite this, he wrapped it closely around his skinny body, sighing.

"It's just fog. Don't create some new fear," he pleaded to himself in an anxious whisper. He felt his face with his fingers to make sure that the features still belonged to him in spite of the cold weather; he was relieved to find them still in their place.

With childlike merriment, the fog rolled freely into the bus station; no one sitting on the benches interrupted its slow spread. The dense mist crept quietly before his eyes, spreading among objects to devour their colors and shapes.

He felt on the verge of passing out; every cell in his body was being forced to dance to the beat of the music being played by the cold.

Equipped with a cigarette, he desperately fought against the cold as he sat on his wooden bench at this late hour of night in the city. As his heart beat with a mysterious fear, he closely watched the fog battalions faintly illuminated by the street lamps. They spread confidently across the station square with little resistance from anything.

He tried to warm his hands by blowing on them. What his heart feared most was this dubious alliance between the night, the cold, and the fog.

Right now, there was nothing in front of his eyes except the darkness and the fog and the silent corpses of buses randomly parked at the station, and he imagined a few ghosts playing in front of him.

Right now, there was nothing in front of his nose except the smell of his coat, the smell of garbage, and the smell of the carts of the street vendors who had left for their stoves at the beginning of the night; there was also the aroma of a steaming pot of tea, which he longingly envisaged.

Right now, there was nothing in his memory, not even any images of a warm female face to rescue his heart from the ambushes that the cold had set up for him.

"If he becomes a journalist then I'll forget all this cold," he said to himself, sighing miserably. He exhaled the smoke of his eternal ally, the cigarette, into the face of the fog.

There were some papers usually used by food cart owners next to his bench. He wearily bent over to pick them up in his trembling fingers. He glimpsed amongst them a colorful hair tie, one of those types that girls used to imprison their locks.

He threw the papers into the wheeled barrel which stood in front of him like a guard protecting his body from the cold breeze. He gazed at the hair tie for a moment then stroked it as a glum smile appeared on his sullen face.

"I found this at the right time," he whispered to himself. "I heard them say in the broom cupboard that in a month or two there's going to be a pay rise. If this is true, I'll have a baby girl." He tucked the hair tie into his shabby coat pocket, imagining it in the hair of a little girl brought to him by a pay rise.

He placed his cigarette lovingly between his dry lips and stood up lazily, scattering his imagined ghosts. Picking up his broom, he began sweeping up the bags, bits of paper and cigarette butts left by people who had traveled to their destinations long ago.

He threw the rubbish into his deep barrel then raised the collar of his coat to his ears and set off, pushing the barrel along in front of him with the feebleness of a burnt-out worker; they both soon disappeared into the fog.

In the silence of his room in the middle of the night the telephone started to ring. His fingers crept idly from under the covers to carelessly pick up the receiver and drag it to his ear. At the other end of the line, he heard the warm voice of a woman. "Good evening, Fadi."

"Nisreen! Good evening . . . But what evening are you talking about? It's nearly morning!"

She laughed softly and said fondly, "I couldn't sleep. I know you stay up till morning with your books and cigarettes, so I said to myself, 'I'll be more generous than Fadi and call him'. So, stingy! I haven't heard your voice for days!"

"I haven't heard my voice for a long time either!"

"Were you sleeping?"

"No, I've just been lying under the covers for hours."

"Reading, of course."

He yawned and replied wearily, "No. I was just thinking."

"About me?" she asked happily.

He rubbed his eyes to expel the long hours of insomnia and said, "Sorry, but I was remembering my childhood."

She was angry for a moment then whispered, "Tell me, what did you remember from your childhood? I love the world of childhood."

"OK, but how much will you pay me for telling you a very interesting story from then?"

"A kiss," she murmured gently.

"I'd prefer a packet of cigarettes," he said in a dry tone.

"You're always so blunt," she replied, trying to hide her annoyance. "As you wish. I'll find a more handsome man to kiss at the university. There are plenty of guys who wish I'd look at them. So I owe you a packet of cigarettes, but please tell me about your childhood."

He leaned his cheek against the palm of his hand on the pillow and said, "I was sad before I went to bed. Did you watch the match?"

"No, I don't like football."

"Lucky you—we lost. After it ended, I didn't feel like reading. I got under the covers to try and warm up then suddenly remembered this one morning when my mom was asleep and my dad was at the textile factory, so I tiptoed my way out to the street . . ."

He stopped and Nisreen asked, "Are you dozing off?"

"No. In the street, I saw the neighborhood children playing football. If you're not going to bring me cigarettes, I'm going to shut up now. I don't narrate my memories to anyone for free."

"Please, tomorrow at the university café, tobacco and coffee are on me. Please, go on."

He removed the covers from his face and went on. "I was clever at that age, but not once had I played football in the street, because of my mother. So I didn't know the rules of the game. Guess what the kids did to me that day?"

"What?" she exclaimed excitedly.

"I hope you bring me king-size *Alhamraa*. That's my favorite tobacco.

"I swear, tomorrow, as we agreed; please carry on," she begged him with more warmth and enthusiasm in her voice.

"They told me—smiling maliciously—to stand behind the goal, and whenever someone kicked the ball out of bounds, I had to run to the end of the street to quickly bring it back to them."

Nisreen laughed joyfully and teasingly, and he sensed childlike mischievousness in her laugh. Through her chuckles she managed to mutter, "They tricked you!"

"Because of my mom, at that time I thought that whoever stood behind the goal to bring the ball back whenever it rolled away was a key and very dangerous player. Those dogs were no smarter than me, but they understood the rules very well because their mothers let them play in the street every day."

Nisreen laughed for a long time again.

"The story isn't over," Fadi whispered.

She stopped laughing and fervently begged him, "Go on."

"The second half is worth nothing less than two packets of cigarettes. I'm not cheating you—that's the price of stories in our local papers."

"You can have four packets, but just keep going, please."

"By chance, my father saw me when he was coming back from his job at the factory. He watched me standing at the edge of the pitch and happily bringing the ball back whenever it rolled away. He got very angry and berated the kids. He dragged me home by the ear in front of them, and my mother started slapping me because I'd dared to get out of her prison."

He stopped talking and the silence lasted for a while. "I'm sorry," Nisreen whispered sorrowfully, consoling him. "I forced you to talk about painful memories, but now your silence is making me regret it."

"I don't know how your mind interpreted what's happening!" he replied indifferently and with an ironic tone. "I was just moving the phone to my other ear and pulling the covers back over me because they'd slipped a bit. The story isn't finished yet."

Nisreen did not say a word, for his answer had surprised her. Fadi coughed and sounded bored as he went on. "My father left the house with a grumpy face, and I stayed alone with my mother's slaps. Half an hour later he came back with a bag in his hand with a new ball inside."

"Oh Lord, a sweet ending."

"It's not finished yet."

"Finish it," Nisreen cried eagerly. "I'm listening."

"What kind of cigarettes do I like?" he asked to reassure himself.

"King-size *Alhamraa*," she answered angrily, so he continued. "On the first night of having the ball, I stayed awake very late, holding it under the covers. I talked to it and warned it about my mom's slaps, and then I went to sleep. In the morning when I woke up, my father was at the factory and my mother was still sleeping. I hugged my ball and crept out of the house. In the street I shouted to the other children and threw the ball to them, then I ran happily behind the goal, where I stood ready."

Nisreen's laughter reached his ear through the receiver. "My memories make you laugh so much," Fadi whispered to her bluntly.

After a few minutes of laughter, she asked him, "Didn't you have any friends when you were a kid?"

"Yes, of course: the wall."

"The wall!"

"Yes, the wall. The wall of the house my mother had us imprisoned in. It was the only one in my childhood who kicked the ball back to me; only the wall played with me."

Fadi heard the sound of a stone hitting his bedroom window.

"Nisreen, I'm sorry, I need to go. My friend's here."

"Friend? Visiting you just before morning—that's strange. What's your friend's name?"

"I don't know."

"Your friend's visiting you, and you don't know his name?"

"I met him by chance a year ago at the bus station. He sat beside me, and we chatted a little."

"And he visits you?"

"Every few days or so."

"As you wish. I've got used to your strange behavior since our first year of uni. Hopefully see you this afternoon at the café. Good night."

"Deal. Same to you, bye."

He hastily dropped the handset back onto the phone and bounded quickly to the window. He removed the pale coat hung over it like a curtain then opened the grille and stuck his head out. He felt a breath of cold air on his face. In the early dawn light Fadi spotted the man with his wheeled barrel under the window.

"Good morning, sir."

"Good morning."

"I passed by here last night, but there was no light on in your room. You fell asleep early for the first time in a year."

"No, I didn't—I was hanging out with my friend in his room. He has a mazut heater. I've only got an electric one in my room, and the old landlady would get angry if she found out that I put it on. She's exhausted me endlessly trying to put up the rent for this bleak, cold room, now that fuel prices have risen."

As Fadi laughed the man smiled wearily and asked, "Do you have any newspapers to give away, sir?

"Of course, with pleasure."

Fadi ducked back into his room for a few minutes that felt like months to the barrel man. He reappeared, thrusting his body out of the window, and tossed down several newspapers rolled up together and tied with a piece of string.

The man picked up the bundle and tucked it inside his shabby coat to protect it from the raindrops that had quietly begun to fall on the streets, devoid of people at the first light of dawn.

"Has your idea convinced him?"

Fadi was asking about the man's son, the one to whom he was taking the newspapers.

The man blew warm air into his closed hands and replied, "Yes, sir. Yesterday evening, he was in the alley playing football with the kids. He came home angry and said to his mother, 'I don't want to be a footballer, I want to be a journalist so I can insult them like Dad's friend does on the pages of the papers.' He might become a journalist like you, sir."

"God forbid," said Fadi with a faint smile.

"Why, sir?" the man asked in surprise.

Fadi leaned a little out of the window and said in a low voice, "In order for him to become a journalist, he must be broken, unhappy and addicted to cigarettes. His life must be full of slaps and kicks. I would hope that his life will be beautiful."

He stopped talking and sighed, then yawned. The man waved farewell to Fadi and turned to his barrel. He pushed it away under the rain that had now started to pour down heavily. No one was in the streets at this hour except him with his barrel and the fog. He did not care much about his appearance, which was that of someone who had fallen in a lake. He walked quietly for a long time, amusing himself by listening to the music played by the raindrops and the wheels of his barrel. He walked along many streets before leaving the neighborhoods of multi-storey buildings and entering the slums with their chaotic and labyrinthine alleys. His exhausted legs carried him along several of these until he reached a near-derelict house. He parked his barrel next to the door, which he opened to enter into a simple room that made up his whole house. The cells of his body started to recover with the warmth that now began to run through his limbs. He took off his dark shoes, hung his coat on a nail in the wall and walked over the old worn plastic mat. His wife was sitting to the right of the wood burning stove; she had gathered in front of her worn out pieces of cloth, some thread and a needle.

"I'll bring you some food," she said to him.

"I'm not hungry," he answered with a grim face as he approached the bed of his young son who was asleep to the left of the stove. His books, jotters, pens, and the remains of an old newspaper were scattered around him. He placed the newspapers under his son's pillow. He brought out the old teapot and put it on the stove then sat down in front of it on the mat with his legs crossed to watch through its holes the slow death of the logs that he felt were smiling foolishly at him, as if their demise did not concern them.

His wife spoke in a hoarse voice, an overwhelming desire to hear his voice exploding inside her chest. "You've been bringing him newspapers since last year. How will they benefit a child like him?"

She held the corner of her headscarf wrapped around her neck and covered her face to protect it from the cold draughts that were stealing through a crack in the windowpane. He wiped his nose with his palm and coughed.

"He loves them; he may become a journalist," he said, still watching the burning logs. He took a voracious drag on his cigarette.

"I saw him smoking with the boys in the corner of the alley yesterday evening."

"It's not a problem, let him do whatever he wants," he said in a cold tone. The colors of the fire were reflected on his sullen features as he contemplated the face of his sleeping son. He took another deep drag on his cigarette and filled the room with its smoke as he exhaled. His wife's mouth turned downwards sadly, and she started tinkering uninterestedly with her needle, thread and pieces of cloth.

As was her habit during her daily life, she traveled with her imagination to warmer places with more words than inside this bleak room whose walls echoed with cold and smoke.

With his imagination, he traveled to clean places where there were no rubbish bins. Neither of them paid any attention to the thick steam rising from the teapot.

One cigarette, a second, a third and then a fourth died on his dry, anxious lips into which the cigarette butts had over time dug deep trenches of invisible wars that he fought daily against worry and its derivatives.

Nothing separated their respective silences but the wood stove and the clouds of tobacco smoke that spread like fog throughout their room.

She coughed a little then turned her face away to escape the smoke. She looked out of the window at the morning rain. After a while, as her eyes wandered despondently over the glass, she sighed and felt a sharp pain in her chest.

She whispered in a suffocated voice that could barely be heard, as if talking to herself; she whispered in a voice colored by a mysterious fear that emanated profusely from the features of her pale face; she whispered quietly and wearily: "Fog out there . . . and fog in here."

There on the wall defaced by cracks were three shabby coats that had no memory, haphazardly hung on their nails, slowly spreading around the room the perfume of ordinary people.

7th November, 2008

"A Life in the Fog"

Taken from the collection *A Damp Cellar for Three Painters*

He had not actually expected the boy to run from his punches and slaps, to rush out of the house and race down the muddy alleys between the run-down houses. Although he beat his children every day, never before had any of them dared to flee. His little son's escape only served to increase his anger and he chased him along the alleys, intending to take him home to thrash him harder.

Some of the neighbors noticed the fat man pursuing his son, waving his stick threateningly, but no one cared because they were all used to such scenes. Hardly a day passed without some father chasing his son to smack him in front of everyone then drag him home like a dog in need of a training session.

On a nearby side street, the terrified boy entered an old building he had spotted. He raced directly down the stairs to the basement and saw a door which had been left ajar. His fear urged him forward to push it open and go through, closing it behind him. He stood there panting.

Turning to look around the room, he gasped in surprise. Statues were scattered all over the place, cold and silent. He walked between them, stumbling over his own feet. He felt as though he had opened a door to the past, to ancient historical eras, like in a story. He suddenly spotted the proprietor of the basement and trembled. He was sitting on an old couch, smoking, and drinking cheap wine.

"Who are you?" he shouted drunkenly at the boy.

Stammering and sobbing, the boy explained that he was hiding from his cruel father and begged the man to allow him to stay.

The basement owner laughed insanely. At that moment, heavy banging on the door caused the boy's heart to sink in panic and fear crushed his soul.

He hurried to squeeze his little body between two sculptures; he crouched down, hiding his face between his forearms in ever-growing terror.

The owner walked heavily to the door and opened it, allowing the father to dash in, cursing. Without greeting the owner, he set about searching in the corners of the basement for his son. The father saw the statues but did not pay them much attention. He walked around the room but did not recognize his son, assuming that he was one of the sculptures. Even the boy felt that he had become a statue as his father passed by; the blood in his veins froze and his heart stopped beating.

When he could not find his son, the father glared at the owner of the cellar as if intending to start a fight to vent his rage. He pinched his nose with his fingers, disgusted by the stink of the cheap wine that filled the place

"And what do you do?" he asked with disdain.

"Me? I'm a sculptor. I made that great statue of the father-leader in the city square twenty years ago. Also, that bust of the son-leader in the public park—I'm the one who made it, three years ago."

Hearing these words—which had mentioned all the country's leaders of the past half century—the father swallowed quietly and dropped his stick. Then he was suddenly smiling widely and bowing to the sculptor, shaking his hand affectionately.

"A pleasure to meet you, sir. I apologize, I didn't recognize you at first. Please excuse me."

He quickly turned, intending to leave this awful hell he had inadvertently entered, but the sculptor called to him from behind: "Wait!"

More terrified than ever, the father turned to him. The sculptor took a swig of wine from the bottle in his hand.

"Have you got any cigarettes?"

"Yes, sir, of course," said the father and he took a packet of cigarettes out of his shirt pocket. He shook it a little to get one out then extended his hand to the sculptor.

The sculptor did not take the cigarette but insolently snatched the entire packet from the father's hand then screamed in his face, "Now get lost!"

The father did not care about losing his cigarettes; he sprinted out of the basement and breathed a sigh of relief when he was back in the alley. He walked home, forgetting all about his son.

Several months passed during which the father did not mention his son or ask whether he had returned. Even the mother had not noticed the disappearance of one of her many children scattered around her in the one small room that made up their entire house.

One evening the father was asleep on the single foam mattress on the floor, his paunch moving up and down regularly with his infernal snores, when his wife shook him by the shoulder. He awoke and turned to her; he was about to give her a slap when he realized that she was gesturing to him to look at the television.

He turned and saw the sculptor there on the screen, but now he was stylishly dressed and smiling graciously for the cameras. Despite the racket his children were making, the father gathered that the sculptor had won a major prize for a statue he had recently completed.

The father did not look at the statue, which was standing next to the sculptor in the middle of the screen. He stared at the sculptor, annoyed, then threw the quilt back over his head to return to his slumber and snores.

The mother, however, kept watching the screen. She was not that interested in the sculptor and his smiles but was staring at the small statue next to him; it depicted a small child, crouching down with his face hidden in his hands.

She felt as though she had seen it before . . . but she could not remember where or when.

She gazed at the television, oblivious to the fact that her baby, who she had been nursing, was hitting her breast with his soft little hand, unable to find a single drop of milk.

6th December, 2013
"Cellar of Sculptures"
Taken from the collection *The Last Friend of a Beautiful Woman*

The torrents of rain ran like stampeding horses, dirty and mud colored. They soon grew tired and gathered in the square to draw upon its paving slabs strange and chaotic figures which would be impossible for even a fortune-teller to interpret. They were the same dark figures that liked to play in his imagination throughout the silent nights.

His recollections were unrelenting and saturated with images that he could not forget. The stub of a cigarette sat neglected between his thick lips; dry lips that belonged to a face formed from melancholy and a touch of mud, a face with features fond of hiding behind a hazy mask that was woven now and always by his cigarette smoke.

His huge body leaning lazily on the door frame, he wearily contemplated the heavy rain, calmly listening to the symphony produced by the collision of the raindrops on the paving of the square.

For hours this rain, whose music added to his depression, had been preventing him from going on his regular nightly visit to the store.

Fifty years had rushed past like autumn leaves being attacked by an unknown storm. During his half-century nothing had managed to sneak over the sky-high walls of his heart, apart from this big screen, which he imagined to be his secret lover—he who had spent his whole life without knowing a woman—and, perched atop the auditorium, his dull room which he had secretly dubbed a country. A country with no national anthem except for the symphony of the rain pouring down onto its roof, and no flag other than his scruffy spare shirt, hung indifferently on the window.

He had not written his memoirs because the events of his life could be summed up in only two lines, half a century of life that had traversed his body without any flavor.

His first and second decades, childhood and adolescence, had been spent in a shanty overcrowded with family in one of the informal settlements of the city. He had never memorized the names of its members, nor they his. The third decade of his life, or the first four days of it, had been spent in the city center. The remainder had passed in a hateful dungeon assigned for those who pulled the teeth out of others without the relevant certification or any licensed or dedicated place to practice, other than the vegetable market. Then, with someone's help, he would go on in the fourth and fifth decades of his life to become the watchman for this semi-deserted cinema in a small square of the old city. He would voluntarily imprison himself among hundreds of films that would help him build his second solitary cell.

He gave up hope that the rain would stop and turned around, entering the auditorium and taking from his pocket a piece of dry bread. He walked up to the window, dipped the bread in a bowl of water and threw it in front of a sparrow that was huddled up in a corner on the stone windowsill where weeks earlier the watchman had made it a humble nest. Now the audience for the evening screening had increased by one to equal, including the sparrow, the number of fingers on one hand.

Every evening the watchman would throw a piece of bread to the sparrow, his cold look suppressing within the bird its desire to tweet thanks to this man.

Through some holes in the window's wooden frame the watchman noticed that the rain had turned to drizzle. He left the sparrow pecking at its food and went out of the building, descending the steps slowly. He passed through the courtyard, empty at this time of night, with a sluggishness suited to his huge body, indifferent to those strangely shaped puddles formed by the rain. He crossed over them like an old and heavily overloaded boat then entered an alleyway, passing by some bins with several rubbish bags scattered around. He heard muffled sounds emerging rom among the bins and imagined the battle now raging between the nice over spoils that would award them one more day of life.

The old seller in the humble shop shook the watchman's hand warmly while the latter extended his own hand in cold silence. The seller had soon tucked into a bag some packets of cigarettes and ready-made food, as if he knew by heart the needs of this obese customer. He handed over the bag and the watchman put some money on the counter and turned around to leave. The seller spoke from behind him.

"I heard from some people that the city council issued an order to demolish the old buildings in the square. They intend to build some wide roads and commercial towers. Did you know about this?"

The watchman turned his face and shook his head indifferently, as if the matter did not concern him. The shopkeeper added, "You know how they are in the municipality. No draft resolution they take will be implemented before ten years are up, and you'll have retired by then."

The watchman shook his head coldly again and left without saying a word. He walked along, greedily dragging on his cigarette, until he reached the bins where he heard a faint noise. He decided to take a look at the mice with whom he had lived for a few days short of a decade in a cramped cell. He approached cautiously, pushing aside the bin bags in front of him with his foot; he bent over to check the dark space between the bins, leaning on the edge of one of them. He bent his huge body over further and nearly lost his balance but grabbed the edge of the bin to stop himself from falling. The bin fell over and rolled away. He looked carefully in the dim glow of the streetlights and spotted two little human shadows among the rubbish bags.

The watchman moved closer; his immense curiosity led him to stretch his neck over the second bin, peering down behind it. He frowned in surprise as he looked at the small and fearful faces of a boy and a girl. They were sitting stuck to the wall hugging their knees to their chests. They curled around each other, frightened to see the face that looked upon them from above, as if their hiding place had been uncovered by his eyes.

"What are you two doing here?" the watchman asked them suspiciously in his dry voice.

The boy replied. "We ran away from our neighborhood this morning. Please, uncle, don't tell our family that you found us." He sounded exhausted.

The watchman hummed and hawed for a few seconds, rubbing his chin with his index finger, then said, "I won't tell anyone, but come with me now—you'll die from the cold out here."

He reached out his huge hands to help the boy and girl stand up, contemplating their pale faces with pity, their bodies tired from the cold, the exhausting journey and hunger, and their worn, dirty school uniforms.

The watchman walked between them, quietly leading them across the square, paved with pale colored slabs, into the cinema. He estimated their ages to be between eleven and twelve. He spat out his cigarette then addressed the boy again, affecting an angry tone:

"And why did you run away?"

"We're neighbors," the boy stammered, his fear making him tremble. "Jumana and I have loved each other since we were little, but when I told my father that I wanted to marry her, he whipped me with his belt, and when her mother heard what I'd said, she imprisoned her with her older sisters and stopped her from going to school for a few days. This morning, I saw her on the way to school and we agreed to escape together. We threw out our books and jotters and ran away."

He said all this quickly then fell silent to catch his breath. He swallowed before mustering the courage to go on. "We decided to escape to the forest and live there forever. We kept walking until the evening, until the rain started pouring down on us, but we hadn't reached the forest, so we hid behind the bins. Uncle, do you know the way to the forest?"

The watchman looked at him in surprise then smiled for the first time in months, which was, in fact, average for him. "What forest are you going to find?" he asked the boy ironically. "You'd need to cross three more cities before reaching the nearest one!"

"Please, uncle, don't take us home!" the boy cried with tearful eyes. "If they see us, they'll kill us. When my older sister, Suaad, eloped with Mr. Aziz, my father and my cousins followed them and killed them. Please, uncle."

The watchman sighed. "Don't be afraid," he said testily. "I'll just take you to my room."

In front of the cinema steps, the boy suddenly cut him off, snatching his hand out of his grip and running off. The watchman stood and shouted to him to come back, but the darkness of the night and the alleys had swallowed up his small body.

The rain gradually began to pour down again. The watchman sympathetically regarded the silent girl then led her to the auditorium and they went up to his room, where he asked her to sit down on the sofa. He bent down in front of the oil burning stove and started messing around with it as the girl's eyes wandered among the pictures hanging on the walls— colorful pictures of different sizes, crowded with elegant men and beautiful women. She smiled and the colors of the pictures enticed her features to shine a little; then she saw the shirt hanging on the window and just below it, on the stone sill, some empty wine bottles and one still half full.

After tinkering with the stove for a few minutes, and despite the decades that had passed since he acquired it, he managed to get it lit.

"You must be hungry," he said gently to the girl. "I'll make you a delicious dinner and hot tea. Don't be afraid of me—from now on, I'll be your new father."

For the first time she opened her mouth and spoke in a shy voice that could hardly be heard, her hands interlaced on her lap. "Uncle," she murmured, "I beg you, bring Yaman back. They'll kill him if they find him."

He sat next to her and kissed her gently on the forehead, a kiss full of parental tenderness. Twenty years of his memory gathering inside its folds hundreds of unforgettable cinematic kisses, and he had finally kissed something: the soft forehead of a little girl whom he was beginning to imagine as his young daughter, he who had never envisaged himself married. Things inside his chest danced primitively. After all those times, places, and lives, he had by chance found a new task for his lips, other than pressing them against cigarettes and bottles of wine.

"Don't worry—he'll come back, I'm sure," he told her confidently, patting her hair gently.

Suddenly, the sound of banging on the main door of the building could be heard. The watchman went down to the auditorium and hurried to the door. He opened it and saw Yaman standing tall in front of the steps, a stone clutched between his fingers.

"Give me Jumana."

"She's sitting beside the stove just now, having something to eat. Do you want her to die of cold on the streets? Throw the stone away and come in." The watchman coughed then added in a sharp irritable voice, "If you could stand a single punch, I wouldn't have exhausted my chest talking to you. Come on, hurry up. I don't want to spend the whole night talking to you in the rain. Come on in."

The boy was confused but he threw the stone away and went up the steps, stumbling over his own feet. Yaman stood fearfully in front of the watchman, who stretched out his hand and put it on the boy's shoulder.

Yaman covered his face with his forearms. "Please, uncle, don't beat me," he begged.

The watchman shook Yaman by the shoulder and pulled his arms off his frightened face. He put his fingers under Yaman's chin, raising his head up, and said, "Don't be scared of me; I'm your friend. Come on, don't try to act like a man when you're still a boy. Come in."

Yaman sat silently on the sofa beside Jumana. The pictures on the wall caught his attention. The watchman switched the radio on then started preparing dinner, swaying to the music—something which was not his usual habit when listening to the radio.

A wave of warmth and reassurance circulated with the blood in their veins. The watchman's large body swaying with his rolled-up sleeves and a towel wrapped around his forehead made them smile. Soon, enthusiasm crept into their bodies, and they started clapping like two sparrows as they sang along to the words of one of the songs resonating around the room. The watchman was content with his whistling which somewhat resembled the song's melody. A voice flashed in his memory, asking, "When was the last time you tried to sing?"

He sighed, ignoring this inner voice as he plated up the food on the table. He did not eat anything himself but lit a cigarette and took a deep drag while looking at the children with a pleasure that revived his soul as they ate ravenously.

Yaman wiped his mouth on the hem of his shirt and said to the watchman, "Give me a cigarette."

The watchman chuckled and said, "I wouldn't advise you to take up smoking. Cigarettes are like the enemy in a battle that'll drag you by the ear to your grave, and you can't resist."

"But, uncle, you smoke a lot—you might die!" Jumana mumbled in a low voice.

The watchman took a long drag on his cigarette and blew the smoke out in rings; they applauded his skill. He leaned toward Jumana and spoke to her in a hoarse voice, sounding as though he were performing on stage:

"Firstly, my little one, I am obese, so no one could drag me by my ear to the grave. Secondly, I won't die easily because I'm like those ancient buildings that you saw in the square. They've been standing there for centuries, and no one has ever thought of dragging them by their ears to the grave, because everyone's afraid of their curse."

He laughed again from amongst the clouds of smoke and Jumana whispered to Yaman, "He's saying strange words." She pointed at the pictures on the wall and added, "Those pictures are strange too. Where did he get his words and pictures from?"

Yaman could not think of an answer, so the watchman told them as he cleaned the table. "My words and pictures are stolen from the films!" he said in a low voice, as if revealing a secret. "For twenty years, I've been watching and learning things from these films, things that we could never find in our city, even if we'd lived here for a thousand years."

A few minutes later they had washed their hands with soap and gone down together to the auditorium. The watchman put the lights on as his guests jumped mischievously over the seats like two butterflies until he called to them, "Look at this."

They turned to where he was pointing and stared silently at a huge, strange machine that was located behind the seats.

"I put the film reel inside and then press the buttons," he explained to them. "A beam of light comes out through the lens and walks softly up to that wall, then it turns into motion pictures, words, music and—"

Jumana rushed up to him and grabbed his hand, interrupting him excitedly. "Uncle, please, let's watch one of your films!"

Yaman clung to the watchman's other hand and begged him impatiently, "My big sister loved movies. Every night she would lie down beside me to tell me the story of one of the films. Show us a film and when I have a job, I'll pay you for two tickets, I swear."

The watchman kneeled down in front of them and put his arms around their necks. "Not tonight," he said. "You're exhausted and it's nearly morning. Tomorrow I'll go down to the basement to search for a good film for you. But be careful—there's an official screening in the afternoon and early evening. After that we'll close the door and watch whichever film we want. You'll have to stay in my room during the screenings, so that no one in the audience sees you and tells your families that you're here. This way, the three of us can avoid getting into big trouble.

"Do a lot of people come here?" Yaman asked, scared by what the watchman had said.

"No," the watchman replied. "Only four or five. It's not because of the film, but for the darkness that lets them kiss each other freely. I keep an eye on them from next to this machine, and they sometimes take a break when actors kiss each other in the film."

The watchman sighed and turned his face away from them. "Everything's permitted in this city except love," he said to himself sadly. "So sometimes two people escape from its nightmare and resort to the darkness of my cinema, but they'll desert their seats here after they get married and after a while others might come instead."

He took a cigarette out of his shirt pocket and lit it. "It's time to go to sleep," he said to them as he tenderly patted their shoulders. "Go up to the room, it's for you. Don't forget our agreement. We mustn't expose ourselves to the danger of people who live outside."

That night the watchman lay down and slept happily, stretched out on the floor behind the seats, beside the machine. When he awoke, he got up quickly and drank a cup of coffee. He went outside and the sunlight hit his body. He felt energized in a way that he was not used to, like a hurricane was circulating in his limbs, pulling him out of his laziness and apathy. He shut the door tightly and went to the market. He wandered around for hours amongst the sellers, bought many toys and sweets, and then returned to the cinema, arriving breathlessly.

He stuck his head around the half-open door of his room and looked at them with happiness that radiated abundantly from his eyes. Yaman was sleeping on the sofa, his left leg dangling down like a boat paddle, while Jumana had cuddled up under the blanket on the bed.

He tiptoed quietly into the room to put the bags on the table then went back out.

He swept the auditorium floor, singing songs composed by his mind on the spot. After the first screening, he went up to them, leaping like a dancer in a manner quite unsuited to his age. He entered the room and was caught in a fit of laughter as he looked at their faces, stained by sweets, and at the chaos that was spread across the room with their scattered toys. This chaos that they had unintentionally created had the aroma of happy music whose rhythm pulled him to dance like a teenager. Jumana and Yaman danced wildly along with him. Sweet laughter rang out.

Three crazy people jumping among the toys, waving their hands in front of their faces, until the watchman fell onto the bed, coughing and panting, and for a few minutes he laughed as he had never done before, as if to compensate for the hundred years that had passed over his features without them raising the slightest smile.

Passing him a glass of water, Jumana shouted, "Which film will we see today?"

The watchman drank some water. "I don't know," he answered. "There are hundreds of films piled up like a maze in the basement. It's no problem; this evening I'll look for a film that'll entertain you."

Then he whispered to himself, "Films won't spoil their innocence." He thought of how he used to cut some scenes from each film to collect inside a wooden box in the basement. Years ago he had named it the Box of the Secret Life of Distant Humans in Cities Beyond the Oceans. He wiped the sweat from his forehead and told them, "I hope to find a film called *Last Tango in Paris* for you—"

"Is it a good film, uncle?" Yaman interrupted.

As if talking to himself the watchman replied, "It's my favorite film. I saw it more than ten times in my first months here. Many things in it resemble my life—the hero even looks a lot like me. I think that if someone watched this film then saw me, they would run up and ask me for an autograph. Anyway, at some point it got lost among the many other reels in the basement, and I didn't have the patience to look for it. I think my memory's forgotten some of its details by now."

He stopped talking to drink the rest of his water, then took a deep breath. "How I miss it," he added absent-mindedly.

He suddenly awoke from his daydreams and bent toward them, frowning. "As we agreed yesterday, it's forbidden to go down to the auditorium until the evening," he warned them.

He took their hands, kissed them then inhaled their scent deeply, saying, "Please don't put yourselves in danger. I love you and I hope that you'll stay by my side forever. This room, the toys, sweets, and films are more beautiful than all the forests in the world. I'll bring you anything you can dream of, but don't leave me alone. Your faces have saved me from solitude. If they find you, I'll be exiled to my loneliness again."

His voice began to quaver during these last words and his eyes filled with salty tears, but none fell; they remained submissive to a long history of imprisonment inside this skull.

Jumana kissed him on the cheek then hugged his neck and said shyly, "We love you too, but we're scared that you'll kick us out of your room, because . . . Yaman accidentally broke one of your plates. We hid the pieces under the bed. Please forgive him."

He forced his features into a smile, then showered their cheeks with many kisses and went silently out of the room. It was time for the second screening. He did not watch any of the attendees or the film, because his mind was painted so brilliantly with the sweet smiles of Jumana and Yaman.

In the evening, he closed the auditorium door and called out to them loudly. They flew down the stairs like two sparrows. He took them down another staircase to the basement, where he picked up a lantern from a shelf next to the door. He lit it and cautiously and slowly entered the dark, spacious room.

This basement, which he had secretly named the Cinema Shrine, contained randomly scattered film reels piled up on top of each other like a maze. He wandered with difficulty among the carcasses of the films, hoping to find that great one that still occupied a corner of his memory, to bring it back to life again. He placed his lamp on the Box of the Secret Life of Distant Humans in Cities Beyond the Oceans. He secretly envied the dusty bodies of the films on which spiders had comfortably spun their webs. He smiled cynically; these corpses could be brought back to life at any time simply by an eye watching them through that huge machine. *Whereas*, he thought as he dusted off some of the reels with his sleeve, *if we were corpses in graves underground, we wouldn't find anyone to bring us back to life.*

Dust had surrounded his nose, and his hands had destroyed many spiders' webs. He came back to the basement door, coughing and holding onto two reels; Jumana and Yaman were eagerly awaiting him, watching him closely.

"I couldn't find *Last Tango in Paris*," he managed to tell them through a coughing fit that had caught him by surprise. "I'll try again another evening. Where could it have disappeared to? It doesn't have legs to run away from this shrine. Anyway, I found these two great films for you."

He spat yellow saliva on the ground and continued, "I chose these two films: *The Woman Next Door* and *The 400 Blows*. They're both made by the same man. Come on, comrades, let's go and watch them."

After the watchman had given his orders to the machine via his fingers, they sat in three adjacent seats in the middle of the front row. The colors of the screen shone on their faces and their eyes absorbed them with boundless joy. They flew on the wings of imagination to other countries.

With wonder, they voraciously devoured the people's stories as they happened on the opposite wall. It was reverence together with awe that washed the hearts of the two small refugees with magic fingers, cleansing them of things that had stuck there from their former daily lives, banishing them to oblivion. The darkness of this auditorium now gave them a freedom they were not familiar with, to smile or grieve, to gasp and tremble without shame or fear of the looks of adults, during a night when everyone apart from the three of them was sound asleep.

This was the first cinema night for the two fugitives—the first of many sweet nights in a festival put together by their watchman friend. Thus, the days of their new lives had another beginning—the moment they heard the creak of the auditorium door closing in the evening, announcing the arrival of the hour for sailing to distant countries from which they would not return until the early morning. From morning until noon they would entertain themselves, eating sweets and playing in the upstairs room, until their bedtime just before the first official screening. As for the watchman, he stopped looking at those attending the two screenings and would instead take a short but intense nap in order to rest his body. He even forgot his only friend—wine—as if he had never even known it. He was now drinking more flavorful wine from two inexhaustible *khabias*: Jumana and Yaman. None of them felt the ancient cinema to be a prison for them, thanks to the countless countries and cities they joyfully discovered every night. The watchman only became angry with them twice; the first time, he was returning from the market when he spotted them throwing cherries at passersby from the upstairs window which overlooked the square. His anger that day exploded like a bomb in their faces, and he blocked the window up with wooden bars, his face dripping with sweat and panic. They had become a treasure that he did not have the slightest desire to lose, even in his imagination—his attachment to them had reached the point of keeping them captive.

The second time was when he caught them messing around in the auditorium, wandering like sheep among the seats during the evening screening. He hastily carried them to his room where he kissed their soft hands and begged them not to do this again, lest anyone see them and tell their families where they were hiding.

Days of unbridled happiness passed. In the evenings the three of them descended to the basement and the watchman entered the maze of films with his lantern, like a sailor fishing for that night's dinner. The pleasure of the colors and words transformed the trio into one family bearing three different surnames. They invented a new game to amuse them-selves as they ate—quoting phrases from the films that had been carved into their memories, imitating the features and voices of other human beings. Every night, they had a date with a pair of beautiful films created in distant cities.

Their entranced eyes flew excitedly over the forests in *The Mirror*. They wished they could give a sweet to the child in *Forever and a Day*. Those same eyes that sighed after *A Time for Drunken Horses* roamed sadly in *The House of the Spirits*, then became ghostly pale for *The Hunchback of Notre Dame* and *Vera Drake*, but they danced cheerfully with *Zorba the Greek*. Yaman wished he were Oliver Twist while Jumana fell in love with *The Piano*.

On another night their eyes withered like thirsty flowers for *The English Patient*, before they climbed together into *Wuthering Heights*. Their eyes also fought with Guevara in *Che* before he left them and went quietly to the other world. Yaman wanted to imitate the moves of Charlie Chaplin on the table but fell on the floor where he lay groaning for a long time. The hammer that shattered Trotsky's head made Yaman's own head ache, and he demise of Frida Kahlo drowned Jumana's eyes in tears.

The nights flowed sweetly by like a stream and the days passed unnoticed; their attention had been hijacked by happiness destined to be imprisoned inside these old walls.

One afternoon, the watchman nodded off beside the projector during the evening screening and fell heavily into a strange dream. He saw himself slowly drowning as he fought against the waves, wailing loudly in a sea upon whose surface unmoving graves were floating. Then two little ghosts appeared on the shore, their features blurry; they threw a long rope to him and started pulling him quietly toward land. His huge body traversed the water from among the graves, and a few meters before reaching the shore he woke up with a start to Jumana and Yaman's hands gently shaking him. He embraced them abruptly, as if he had not seen them in years. He hugged them tightly to his chest, groaning in a muffled voice, parental instinct emanating from his features.

He came back to them at the basement door, blowing dust off the film reels he was carrying. Before he could utter a word, Yaman spoke: "'I haven't found *Last Tango in Paris*,'" he said, imitating the watchman's voice reciting his daily phrase.

A childish grin appeared on Jumana's face. Yaman smiled at her and winked then warned the watchman, "We won't tell you our secret until you find *Last Tango in Paris*."

The watchman laughed and bowed to them. "Well, I've found you *Pierrot the Madman*, *The Extras*, and *Autumn Sonata* as well," he said.

Jumana and Yaman jumped and cheered, clapping their hands. Tonight they would have a big and hearty meal that would surely sate their appetite. A few minutes later they had set sail alongside this feast and did not finish it until the afternoon of the second day. They got in some rest, sweets, and play between the three screenings.

The watchman escorted them to the room where Yaman lay down on the sofa and Jumana on the bed, yawning. They were very tired after the three films they had just brought back to life. The watchman tucked them in, showering them in fatherly love that shone abundantly from his eyes. He tenderly kissed their foreheads then waved goodbye as he stood at the doorway. They waved back to him. He went out and closed the door but remained standing outside the room. He took a deep breath and closed his eyes, leaning his forehead against the door. He exhaled heavily, biting his lip. "If only I had found you two years ago," he said to himself.

He opened his eyes, and his gaze sank into the wood of the door as he imagined the sweet slumber of the boy and girl. After a moment, he wrote 'CLOSED FOR MAINTENANCE' on a piece of paper and hung it on the door of the auditorium. He slept between the seats for a few hours. When he awoke, he stretched and yawned, got up and quickly left the cinema to go to the market. The sky was cloudy and foretold approaching rain.

From the vendors with their shouts that vexed even the stones, he bought Jumana and Yaman all the clothes they had asked for last night. He had recorded all their wishes on a scrap of paper secretly under the table because he did not want to spoil the surprise he was preparing, which was now hiding in the bags among the voices of the sellers.

He bought many things he never imagined he might go to market for. Many beautiful items suitable for his friends' ages that he himself had not seen in his own childhood. When he had finished, he hurried back to the cinema, his imagination painting the inside of his head with images of the surprise that would spring up and dance on the faces of Jumana and Yaman when they saw the clothes.

The cold winter evening fell with its dark cloak, like a *marid* from its sky train, onto the streets and neighborhoods. Cold air blew on the watchman's face, and he was unable to protect it because his hands were full with the bags. The daylight faded completely to be replaced by dim streetlamps.

As he climbed the steps of the cinema, he looked up. He could not see the moon, for it had been caught by thick clouds which had thrown it carelessly behind them as they watched the earth with lust, indicating their overwhelming desire to take over the streets with rain. A mysterious fear rose in his chest for a second.

Panting, he threw the bags onto some seats in the auditorium and planted a cigarette between his lips. He lit it, took a drag and blew out the smoke. He ascended the stairs wearily and went to his room. He stuck his head around the door and silently contemplated the two angelic faces sleeping deeply there.

He sat a while in the auditorium, awaiting their awakening. Boredom gnawed with sharp fangs at his mood, and he became impatient. A thought suddenly came to his mind, blowing up all the soldiers of boredom who had been besieging his temper without mercy.

He went down to the basement with his lantern, alone this time. He walked between the mountains of film reels to the other end of the room, where he crouched down and started to turn them over carefully.

The minutes slowly passed. He could smell the dampness of the place and hear the dreary monotonous rhythm of the rain falling outside. He picked up a reel and stared at it in disbelief, then laughed as he read *Last Tango in Paris*. He hugged it to his chest and hurried out of the basement, stumbling over the other reels, stirring the dust that covered them and enraging the spiders who had been subjected to many massive massacres over the past few days.

He sat on a seat, contemplating the film reel happily. He used his sleeve to wipe away the dust that had accumulated over many years, then planted a long kiss on the reel which would have satisfied many a charming woman. He embraced the reel as if it were a small child.

"They won't wake up for ages," he said to himself as he looked up at the staircase leading to his room. "They went to sleep late. Why don't I watch the film? I can watch it again with them when they wake up."

He patted the film reel and went on, "I feel like my memory's been cheating me in recent years. Some of the details of this film are almost totally missing."

Happy with his plan, he washed the dust and sweat from his face and gulped down a quick cup of coffee. He fitted the reel into the machine to bring the story hidden inside it back to life. He messed a little with the audio to increase the volume, aiming for maximum enjoyment of his favorite film, its dialogues and its music.

He chose a seat in the middle of the front row then sat down and relaxed. During the opening credits, he felt his shirt pocket to make sure he had his packet of cigarettes and was reassured to find it there.

The watchman gazed intently at the screen, watching the scenes as if giant invisible hands were stretching out to pull him and his cigarettes into the story being narrated through the shots and scenes, flowing in a rhythmic way that spread warmth throughout the recesses of his heart. His mind swung like a pendulum between snatches of memory of his life and the scenes in this film, numbing the cells of his body as if he were a wounded man on the operating table.

His tongue tirelessly repeated aloud various expressions of concern and fascination, until, like a drunk poet, he started unintentionally ad-libbing words and phrases uttered by the actors or after a scene left his huge body shaken. He was indifferent to the storm which was lashing violently against the door. Perhaps someone would open the door for the wind to enter the auditorium like a refugee escaping the loneliness of the alleys outside.

During the final scenes he was disturbed a little by some noises that the audio system started transmitting along with the sounds of the film. They resonated in the darkness of the hall and the roar of the storm, and he determined to fix it after the remaining minutes of the film's life.

With nerves tight as guitar strings inside his limbs, the watchman sadly contemplated the face of the film's protagonist, which so strikingly resembled his own. The watchman shouted a warning to him, but the hero on the screen paid no attention either to this or to the gun in the heroine's hand. A shot was heard in the auditorium. The hero's features convulsed and were distorted by pain, the same features that twisted in pain on the watchman's face. This was followed by two more gunshots, louder than the first.

The hero inside the screen sprawled on a balcony overlooking the old Parisian neighborhoods, and next to him lay the soul of the watchman as he regarded the scene, holding his breath. Then the hero died there on the balcony, his knees drawn up to his chest like a sleeping child.

The screen dissolved to black, the soundtrack faded, and a weighty silence hung over the darkness of the auditorium. The creaking of the door brought him to his senses. The watchman clapped his hands emphatically three times. He took a drag on his cigarette and murmured, "How wonderful that film is. I'd only forgotten a few minor details at the end of it."

The noise of the door had disturbed his euphoria. He walked toward it. "Damn every door that allows the winter wind to mess with it," he said angrily, as if he were in a film himself.

He closed the door, noticing that the storm had departed and the rain had stopped. "Time to wake them up," he whispered to himself. "They'll be so happy with the clothes and the film."

He picked up the bags from the back seats and went up to the room. When he reached the door, he lifted the bags to cover his face then burst in, singing a funny song that he had learned from them, making enough racket to wake the sleepers in their cave. He stood with his face hidden behind the bags imagining the surprise now drawn on their faces. But nothing was happening—only silence welcomed him, extending its emptiness into the watchman's ears. He grumbled about their long sleep today then lowered his forearms awkwardly to his chest to prevent the bags from falling, and his lips tautened with surprise as he looked between the bed and sofa; no one was lying on either one. The emptiness he had heard upon bursting into the room was now visible to him, looming over the furniture.

"The troublemakers, they've hidden under the bed as usual," he whispered to himself, and he craned his neck over the bags. As they fell to the floor, he let out a gasp of immeasurable terror as a horrific bomb of fear exploded across his features. He staggered backwards, banging into the door. His knees trembled violently; his legs seemed to age within a second and could no longer hold him up. His body slowly sank down to lie crumpled beside the door like a huge heap of worn rags. He raised his hands and slapped them over his eyes, refusing to believe what he had just seen, but in the darkness of his closed eyes he could still see Jumana and Yaman's bodies, thrown randomly next to the table. Blood poured heavily from two holes in their heads, drawing on the floor a strange and chaotic form, impossible for even a fortune-teller to interpret.

He opened his eyes and turned his face away. He wanted to cry, to shout, to hit his head against the wall, to impale a sharp knife in the chests of all human beings. His cells were ravaged by a mute paralysis that had the flavor of impotence and bewilderment, whose massive iron bells started clanging, a huge deafening echo, inside his head. He covered his ears with his palms as he writhed in pain across the door. Feeling like he was suffocating, he tried and tried to not believe that the death train had just passed through the room, stopping at the station to collect two passengers before continuing on its way. He did not want to believe what he was seeing, but his eyes, withered like a flower plucked from its branch, made him release long groans that raged like a passing storm in the room.

He covered his eyes again, glimpsing in the blackness buildings collapsing, planes falling, bombs exploding and a speeding train, accelerating without a whistle, running over in less than a second the two little shadows trying to pull him from the sea of graves. He took a deep breath, opened his eyes, and looked again—perhaps something would have changed. Their faces were pale blue, and he remembered once reading on a subtitle in one of the films that this blue was the color of the faces of passengers to the other world. This pale blue color had removed their lives from their bodies and helped them to ascend to heaven.

Paralyzed, he crawled toward them on his knees, crossing the bizarre bloody shape drawn on the tiles. He pulled them up to hug them to his chest; their heads were loose and lolled carelessly and apathetically. His body began to sway like a clock pendulum, his grief and pain making him hallucinate like a madman.

"Don't leave me alone. We agreed to live together forever. It's not fair that you leave, and I remain alone. I'd got used to you here. I beg you, come back. We still have so many films to watch together. Please, I don't want to return to my loneliness."

Dead grim silence reigned. He squeezed their heads to his, closing his eyes as he smelt their faces and the stench of death spread in his lungs. He groaned and heard a warm voice in his ear.

"We told you we wanted to go to the forest! Why didn't you show us the way?"

"The forest was far away, and I didn't know where it was. Forgive me," he murmured sorrowfully as he was slaughtered by his remorse, and the warm voice touched his face again, saying, "We'll tell you our secret. Oh, how hard we tried until we found you; we roamed the streets and the neighborhoods for years searching for you, until we found you by the bins. We only wanted to tell you about your mother's will. That night, we were sitting by her head minutes before she died. She was all alone, no one was near her. She begged us, crying, to search for you to tell you—"

The voice disappeared for a second then came back, this time in his old mother's tone. "Years have passed, and I haven't seen you. Are you OK? I'm worried about you, I miss you so much. I love you so much."

He felt a bitter pain in his throat and tightened his grip on the two heads so that their faces touched either side of his nose. He breathed in their smell deeply. The warm voice whispered to him again in the tone of a young child. "If you love us and love your mother, come with us. Don't stay alone like this. Come with us. There are plenty of films in that world in which we can be the heroes."

The voice stopped, then quietly spoke again, this time in the tone of a cold, dead body. "When the leaves fall in autumn, show them where our grave is, so they may cover us up to protect us from the cold winter."

He moaned in pain. The voice spoke again, and this time it had a tone similar to his own. "Aren't you already late?" it asked him. "How long will you be? Try to migrate from this life; try, you may succeed."

The watchman raised his head and groaned again. The voice, which had sounded warm, cackled and now put on the tone of death. "There are no vacant seats on tonight's journey to the other world," it chanted mockingly. "You're going to stay here forever, here where no one loves anyone."

He opened his eyes and got up like a hundred-year-old man, not knowing where to go. He felt on the verge of suffocation and tore his shirt from his chest. He hurled several hard punches at the wall, making the pictures fall and calmly land on the two dead faces. He picked up from the windowsill his half-full bottle of wine, left forgotten there for days. He thirsted for ordinary wine now that the two *khabias* had run dry. The jars whose sweet wine had so intoxicated him these past few nights.

He staggered downstairs in his blood-stained clothes, hitting the walls as he passed by. He walked to the door of the auditorium and exited the cinema in a daze. His head spinning, he sat in the darkness on the bottom step overlooking the square. He downed his wine in a single gulp. Under the dim lights on the square, he watched a drop of blood trickling down his palm to the tip of his index finger then fall into one of the strangely shaped puddles. The watchman silently contemplated their weird, dark forms that had been drawn by the rain on the paving slabs. He fancied them ghosts, sniggering loudly.

He wiped his face with his hand, smearing it with blood. "The sound system wasn't broken," he said decisively and with much regret. "The noise was the killers'."

A salty tear breathed a sigh of relief as it burst from his eye and flowed down his cheek, bidding farewell to a cell upon whose edge it had long teetered. He lit a cigarette and blew out the smoke in front of his face. "The winter wind can't open a heavy door, no matter how strong it is," he added loudly, his words resonating across the square. "My memory didn't betray me—I betrayed it. I knew that the hero of *Last Tango in Paris* is killed with one shot, but I didn't know that the timing of the killers who slipped into my room would be so similar to the timing of the killer in the film."

A ribbon of images of Jumana and Yaman played across his memory. The first picture showed them as they sat frightened behind the rubbish bins . . . The last image showed them tossed carelessly on the floor as their blood drew its strange shapes on the tiles. He stood up like a mythical beast, flinging his cigarette away. He stared wrathfully at the old buildings around the square, cursing them with hatred and spitting at them, only to hear his insults echoing back as half of his spit dribbled down his chest.

The old buildings that had stood for centuries on the edge of this small square did not care about his insults or spit, so he hurled his empty wine bottle at them—maybe this would succeed in killing them. He had a fit of coughing then screamed into the night of the square, attempting to rile the old buildings which were now giggling in his face. "No!" he shouted with all his strength. "They didn't die! It's not real, I'm just imagining that they were killed. Yes, they're alive and they're going to wake up now and watch *Last Tango in Paris* with me."

He left the door of the auditorium wide open and ran wildly to his room, animal-like sounds erupting from his throat. He bent over the bodies and lifted them up, throwing the first corpse over his right shoulder and the second over his left. He went out of the room and descended the stairs. On the staircase he tripped and fell over the bodies. They rolled and tumbled down on top of each other all the way to the bottom, but he stood up like an unbeatable fighter, picking them up again and taking them into the auditorium. He sat Jumana and Yaman down on two adjacent seats in the middle of the front row. He left them there while he went to turn on the projector to bring *Last Tango in Paris* back to life.

He threw his body on a seat next to them in front of the big screen upon which colors were starting to appear. He groped in the pocket of his torn shirt and breathed comfortably as he lit a cigarette. During the film, he had a mysterious feeling that those strange dark shapes drawn on the ground by the accumulated rain were crouched heavily on his chest. They were widening and growing ever bigger.

A few meters behind them, on the stone sill of the window, the sparrow shook the rain from its wet feathers, shivering with cold. It started to chirp and twitter. It had been doing this every few hours over the past few days because its friend had stopped throwing it any wet bread crumbs, specifically since his two guests had come along and caused the watchman to forget about the sparrow completely, leaving it a prey to hunger.

With an empty stomach the sparrow gazed at the backs of those three heads for a few minutes. The colors of the screen cast a shadow over the heads that sat mesmerized in front of it. The sparrow chirped again loudly, calling out in vain to its friend as knives of hunger bled it of its voice. The little bird took off desperately through a hole in the wooden window frame, soaring among the trees around the square. The sun was rising and starting to shine above the square, and a few people crossed it silently as they hurried to work.

The sparrow could not see anything to feed on from above the square's paving slabs. It sighed and flew on until it arrived, exhausted, at a deserted garden. It explored the trees for a long time, hoping to find something to eat, but to no avail. It fell asleep on the trunk of an aging tree and woke up after a while to the din of hunger cutting through its body from the inside with a rusty blade. The sparrow hung on as long as it could then flew off stiffly. The sun had risen to the middle of the sky like it did every day by this time when the sparrow landed on the branch of an upright tree next to the square, a headache disturbing its vision. However, it could still see a crowd of people in front of the cinema.

The old owner of the store hobbled by, leaning on his crutch and manoeuvring his way with difficulty through the overabundance of cars parked alongside the pavement. He looked at the people jostling noisily in front of the cinema door. He contemplated them in surprise for a moment for it had been decades since such a crowd had gathered there!

"They must be showing a really good film today!" he whispered in amazement as he scratched his nose, wondering which one it was.

He stepped onto the pavement, unaware that something had fallen off the tree he was standing next to and landed on the edge of the pavement.

The old man curiously raised his head, craning his neck. He saw the cinema door open, the clamoring crowd in front of it, voices and words overlapping like a chaotic dust storm. The messy crowd of people had spread in waves from the door of the cinema, down the steps and all the way to the middle of the square. Then they started gasping and moving away from the door in panic.

The old man looked on more closely, taking a step forward and trampling unknowingly on whatever had fallen from the tree a moment ago. He stood on his tiptoes and could see men with silent faces dressed in white gowns, slowly coming out of the cinema, carrying three bodies between them on rickety stretchers with worn covers.

The heavy weight of one of the corpses was causing some annoyance to one of the orderlies, who secretly cursed his meager monthly incentive.

18th August, 2009
"The Cinema Watchman"
Taken from the collection *A Damp Cellar for Three Painters*

Like a ballerina who had mastered the art of moving gracefully across the tiles, the young waitress tirelessly distributed cups, dishes and smiles with unparalleled enjoyment. She moved between the customers' tables, light as a butterfly, smiling softly, her slender body swaying to the tunes played on the radio.

The features of her fresh face revealed that she was around 18 years old. In a black skirt and a pink shirt, she had been working in this humble restaurant with its elderly owner, who was an old friend of her mother's, for a year. Alongside her father's pension, her salary supported a family which included a diabetic mother and a father who had served four decades in the navy. He had retired a few months ago to devote himself fully to his favorite hobby: collecting carton cigarette packets which he glued together into various forms. He was the only one, both within the family and amongst their visitors, who could see any meaning in these shapes. Three younger sisters were still studying and an only brother had not yet started school. Their mother described the son as her bird and their father had lovingly nicknamed him The Captain. His sisters, on the other hand, described him as the worst swimmer they had ever known because every day he liked to say good morning to them as follows.

They would approach his bed on tiptoes, full of suspicion and fear. One of them would take hold of his duvet and, after a few moments of apprehensive silent prayer, remove it, revealing a wide wet patch on the white sheets under the middle of his body. They would let out groans and sighs, fed up with life with this brat.

This morning, they saw that the wet spot had doubled its radius. They felt as if he was brazenly challenging them, so the four of them decided, as they gathered around his bed, to tear him limb from limb, especially when he opened his eyes and said an innocent "Good morning" to their sullen and angry faces; he had gone too far in his consistent attempts to make the sheets dirty.

At that moment their mother rushed to his bed and hugged him to her chest. She managed to persuade her daughters to postpone the implementation of their idea for a few years until he had grown up a little, since God does not accept into His paradise a child who has not yet learned the alphabet. She kissed him. They reluctantly agreed and moved away from his bed as he stuck his tongue out at them and secretly vowed never to learn the alphabet, no matter how much his sister explained it to him in the evening.

The 18-year-old girl soon forgot her brother's morning gifts; she hastily hurled his sheets into the washing machine then dressed and went to the restaurant, where she would stay until the end of the evening. Her academic fortune had not been good, but she did not lament this: during a visit to them at home, the old friend of her mother's had contemplated her slender figure and offered her work in her small restaurant for a decent wage. She and her mother had accepted the offer. Her father had no opinion because the cigarette packets had kidnapped his mind to a world of shapes incomprehensible to all but him.

At the end of each month's work, she devoted a good portion of her salary to buying various kinds of laundry powder to clean the treacherous stains her brother liked to inflict upon his clothes and sheets. She also put aside a sum to buy novels that she loved to read to her sisters as they gathered around the oil-burning stove in the evenings, listening intently to her voice while their father sat at the nearby table upon which he had piled his empty packets. He examined them in great depth, stroking his chin, while the mother listened to the story as she sat on a chair beside them, knitting a jumper for her little son—the son who always took the opportunity of his sisters' preoccupation with the story to deliberately drink as much water as he possibly could, even if he was not thirsty.

The restaurant clock hanging on the wall above the head of the old woman, who was reading a novel the young waitress had brought to her that morning, struck four p.m. The waitress had been humming as she moved amongst the tables, watching the clock eagerly as the minutes dragged like hours, when a stranger entered the restaurant. As soon as the waitress spotted him, she gasped quietly with joy. It was a gasp of love that had been growing in her heart secretly and silently since the first time this stranger had come to the restaurant three months before. His tall figure, Middle Eastern olive skin, sad features, and fine moustache had seduced her. Over the past three months this stranger had come in every day at four o'clock in the afternoon, give or take a few minutes. He entered the restaurant with his grim face exuding depression and fatigue, then sat without a word at a table located next to the window overlooking the street. He never changed this habit, to the extent that most of the other restaurant goers secretly called it 'the stranger's table'. No one else even approached that table anymore. Two girls had accidentally sat there one evening, but the waitress politely asked them to move because it was booked, and the pair had apologized and sat elsewhere.

On that day she had been afraid that he would not come, but as soon as four o'clock arrived, he entered as always, grim and silent, to sit as usual at his table, scattering his newspapers messily upon its surface. Within minutes he had eaten a simple meal, had a glass of wine and lit a cigarette, glancing neutrally at passersby in the street. Before finishing his cigarette he threw some cash on the table. He tucked his newspapers under his arm and left as he had entered: sullen, silent and in haste. He never bothered to look at her as she asked him in a whisper what he would like to eat, or when she bent to place his order on the table, hoping that his eyes would find her face; instead, his eyes always wandered among the words on his newspapers before the food came and were fixated on the window afterward. It was for this reason that she harbored a formidable enmity toward newspapers and windows, but she did not hate him. She wished with a quiet grief throughout those months that he would give her one look, but he entered and left as if she did not exist. Not that this disregard and indifference toward her at all diminished the love that had exploded in her heart when she had first seen him. It had grown inside her over the passing days until by the end of the third month it had flourished into a tree upon whose branches birds perched along with the laundered clothes of her brother. She did not understand why she was in love with him, with his inscrutable, bleak demeanor. What she did know was that sweet feelings flowed abundantly in her chest when she shyly approached his table, listening in confusion to the beats of her heart, afraid that one of the diners at the nearby tables may hear. She soon became addicted to looking in his direction from wherever she was among the tables when he was there.

Last night, lying in bed in the darkness of her room, she had talked intimately about him to her sister, describing him as she saw him in her imagination. After an hour she fell silent, realizing that her sister had fallen asleep before hearing anything she had said. Another evening last month she had overheard the whispers of three restaurant goers who were sitting some way from the stranger's table. As she leaned over to put the cups down for them, one of them looked closely at the stranger and said to his friends, "That stranger fled his country and came here half an hour after a coup had taken place there. The new rulers in his country are urging our government to expel him, otherwise they're going to expel our ambassador from their capital." He stopped to drink some water then added confidently, "He seems to be an important man in his country."

The days passed with the whispers of others, the ambiguity of the stranger and her shy and infatuated stolen looks. Three months of heartbeats that could only be heard at four o'clock on those autumn afternoons.

This afternoon, however, fell on her differently. The stranger came into the restaurant at the usual time, uncharacteristically abrupt and unusually loud. He was whistling some melody and swaying like a drunk to his own rhythm. Then, like an actor on a stage, he bowed to the other customers, his face shining with joy, and took off his hat. Despite their amazement at this sudden transformation in his features and behavior, the customers showered the stranger with welcoming phrases. Even the waitress, who had gasped happily at his entrance, was completely taken by surprise and stood hugging her small tray to her chest. He put his hat back on, angling it to hide his eyes from everyone, then strutted around like a dancer, tucking the fingers of one hand into his belt and waving the other as he hummed a famous song. People started clapping excitedly, applauding his dancing walk until he reached the waitress, whose white feet he had spotted tucked inside her soft shoes. He lifted his hat slightly off his forehead and looked at her. She was greatly confused and turned her face away a few times for fear that her eyes might meet his. She tried to step away, but her legs betrayed her, and she remained mesmerized in front of him, her features betraying her confusion. A red hue crept into her cheeks. Her body shuddered and she let out a startled cry as the stranger suddenly grabbed her by the hand and pulled her to his chest. Her eyes were wide and fearful, and her tray fell to the floor. For a moment she did not understand what was going on as the stranger pulled her arm up, throwing it like a scarf over his shoulder and around his neck. Then he hugged her, wrapping his arms around her waist to dance with her like a lover with his beloved in a film. She swayed her tense body against his. However, the applause of the customers who were enjoying the scene, the loud singing of some, the standing ovation of others beside their tables as well as the old owner's giggles as she sat on her chair by the door, turning up the radio on her table as her shoulders shook—all added a rare and pleasant hustle and bustle to the restaurant's atmosphere. All of these things surrounded her body and forced it to surrender, to flow in captivating movements like a gypsy whose body colluded with the music of an old guitar, spreading its soul to her delicate waist. These few minutes were enough to turn the restaurant into a wedding venue; some of the customers and their sweethearts started dancing together beside their tables, the semi-collective singing, the sweet laughs of beautiful girls, the giggles of men and the old woman, the music flowing from the radio. The waitress could not believe what was happening; this was much more than she could have hoped for over the past three months. Her body tenderly touched his, then they moved apart only to come together again. Two bodies that did not know each other's names revealed in that narrow space a dance that revived her soul; she swayed while leaning on his shoulder with an ecstasy that she had never felt before in her life. As she contemplated the stranger's Middle Eastern features that had so captivated her heart, she felt as if two small wings made of jasmine and carnations had sprouted from her back, enabling her to fly freely, dancing above the seas and forests while migrating birds landed on her shoulders, as if she were in a dream she wished would never end.

The party, which had begun without planning or prior intention, soon calmed down and was extinguished, having revived the souls of everyone present, young and old.

The stranger started panting. Sweat broke out on his forehead then a sharp coughing fit hit him. He laid his hand on his heart and groaned for a second. He managed a brief smile as he held her hand, squeezing it gently. He took off his hat and humbly bowed to the audience. A round of applause made the waitress bow too and her heart almost escaped from her chest to fall on the tiles.

The stranger turned and gazed at her. A loud voice rang out from the crowd, commanding the stranger, "Kiss her!"

With eyes that hid many secrets in their depths, the stranger gently contemplated her warm eyes as they played music of happiness and beauty. She glimpsed inside the depths of his eyes hazy pictures and stories from his life. He leaned toward her cheek and smelt her scent deeply, holding his breath to keep her perfume inside his lungs. Even the customers held their breath as they watched. After a while, which felt like an eternity to her, he kissed her on the cheek with a grace befitting a butterfly. She felt lightheaded, as if she could almost faint; she had never felt anything like it in all her years. Everyone clapped enthusiastically, shouting *Hooray!* and smiling at the scene which lured their imaginations into dreams of their own kisses and stories in which they were the heroes. The stranger waved to them, laughing. As for the waitress, she flew like a bird with a mouth that showered the faces of others with shy smiles as she held her hand to her cheek, as if trying to protect her first ever kiss of love. She then sat on a chair next to the old owner, blushing.

The stranger walked toward his usual table, coughing. A man at a nearby table handed him his half-full glass of wine. The stranger grabbed it and raised it in front of the watching customers. They too raised their hands, some with glasses of wine, some with cups of tea, others with coffee, and one with a glass of water, the same man who had given the stranger the wine. Everyone drank to the stranger's toast, and he downed his wine in one gulp then reached his table by the window. Exhausted, he collapsed onto his chair. He lit a cigarette and exhaled sharply, then tugged at the buttons of his shirt to release his neck from its captivity. His collar was completely drenched in sweat.

One of the customers jumped up from his chair with his huge body, shouting in a hoarse voice and raising his fist high: "Hey, beautiful waitress! Put some glasses of wine on all the tables—it's on me this evening."

He then thumped his chest like someone seducing a damsel in distress. He pulled a face of humility as words of thanks and praise poured in from all directions from the people sitting in the restaurant, some of them applauding him for his hospitality. His backside was about to touch his chair when he stood up again, his face full of panic like someone who had suddenly awoken from a stupor. "Oh, and lovely waitress," he shouted beseechingly. "Please make sure it's a cheap one."

Some people laughed, some smiled, others mocked him, and some were annoyed. As for the big man, he sat down, indifferent to the fact that the number of girls showering him with admiration following his first offer had now decreased to zero. His mind was no longer on them, but on his pocket.

The young waitress peeked at the stranger from a distance. A second coughing fit hit him, more severe than the first. He used many tissues as he coughed. She inclined her head and stared gloomily at the tiles. She sighed as her imagination strayed. "Does he love me?" she murmured to the old woman.

The old woman leaned toward the waitress and patted the locks of hair that flowed to the middle of her back and were as black as coffee. "Yes, my little one," she answered confidently. "He's deeply smitten with you and has fallen madly in love. He'll never find a more beautiful girl than you, not in his own country and not in ours!"

The waitress's rosy lips stretched into a smile. Then with an expression of wonder she asked, "But where did all his sudden happiness come from? He's always sullen and frowning."

The old woman thought for a few moments, scratching her head, then said, "It seems that he was listening to the news on the radio before he came here. He must have heard some news that his friends back home had succeeded in carrying out a new coup and—"

"That means he'll return to his own country!" The waitress interrupted fearfully.

"Of course he'll return, to become a minister or—"

"But if he goes back, what will I do?" the waitress interrupted again.

The old woman smiled and winked at her. "You'll have to become hooked on listening to the news, just like my husband," she replied, "until one day, hopefully not too far off, you hear that another coup has toppled this stranger and his group, and he'll be back in here before you even arrive."

The old woman fell silent then exhaled. After a while, she went on in a tone packed with decades of life experience. "Strangers are like this. They don't change their habits: they appear suddenly to kidnap our hearts with their charming eyes, and before we know anything about them, they disappear, just as suddenly, having stolen part of our soul. Many strangers may appear in your life, but you're like all other women—you won't learn this lesson well. Women are like this—ages have passed and their souls are still being kidnapped by strangers. What upsets me most, my daughter, is that INTERPOL takes care of so many other issues, but not this one!"

The old woman laughed, but seeing fear in the eyes of the waitress, who had turned pale after these words, she added some advice: "Go and sit at his table; talk with him a little, ask him about his life, about his family, about the things he loves and the things he hates, and how he got here. Get to know the tone of his voice. I'll fill the customers' orders until you're back."

"I can't!" the waitress blurted out in a low voice.

Then, as if she had found the perfect solution, she said happily, "I'll write him a letter and put it in with that *fatayer* dish he always eats."

She stood up quickly without waiting to hear what the owner thought of this idea and ran to the kitchen. The old woman's memory had been captured by the idea of the letter, taking her back to the past years of her life.

The waitress entered the small kitchen and closed the door. She took a pen and small notebook out of her blue shoulder bag which was hanging on a hook. She sat on a chair, flipping her notebook pages angrily as she saw her little brother's Picassoesque sketches on the paper. She breathed a sigh of relief as she found a page which had not been destroyed by these strange and chaotic forms that her brother was so good at drawing; he often drew dozens of them within minutes. She pressed her knees together and hunched over the white paper. Taking a deep breath, she spontaneously started writing, reading the words she improvised as she wrote them down.

"Good evening to the man with the calm face and deep eyes! I apologize, for I don't know your name, nor which country you're from. I only know the color of your eyes. This is the first letter I've ever written to a man. My cousin wrote many letters to her lover, but she's not here to help me. I've been watching you for three months and I feel that I liked you from the first time you came to our restaurant. However, you never paid any attention to me, and you didn't try to look at me even once, until today. You made me sad through the long nights.

"It seems that you went to hospital this morning and had a successful operation on your eyes. Thank you for that fun dance. I have an idea: tomorrow's a holiday and in the evening the cinema is showing a wonderful film which I saw two years ago with my sisters. I'm sure you'd like it. If you love me as the owner of the restaurant tells me you do, I'll meet you tomorrow evening in front of the park, so we can go together and watch the film. Would that be OK? If you love me, blow me a kiss—I'll be looking at you. If you don't, then gently tear up this letter and throw it out the window with tenderness, so that it falls on the heads of people in the street like snowflakes.

"P.S. I won't write my name until I know yours.

"P.P.S. Please stop smoking. You remind me of my grandmother's fireplace, and I fear for your health. Were it not for these damned cigarettes you could have danced with me until midnight, but that cough kidnapped you. Thank you for the beautiful dance; I've never felt such happiness as I did while you were dancing with me.

"P.P.P.S. Do you prefer *za'atar fatayer* or cheese ones?"

She folded the paper the way she would usually fold a favorite piece of fabric, then held it between her hands and pressed it to her chest. She raised her head a little and closed her eyes. She sighed and then started praying in a low voice from the bottom of her heart. "Lord, please, I beg you, lengthen and protect the life of this stranger's government forever. Oh Lord, do not allow his riotous friends to succeed in overthrowing it. Oh Lord, it is a pious and kind government. Lord, please help this government arrest all the friends of this stranger. Lord, I do not want them to be hanged, but I want them to be imprisoned forever, so that this man can remain a prisoner of my heart. Lord, I beg you, take all the remaining years in the life of our government, and give them to the life of this stranger's government, because his government worships you every day. Please make my wish come true. Please also help my little brother because I do not want to spend the rest of my life washing his clothes and sheets every day. Please Lord, I do not want anything more than this."

She fell silent then took a deep breath and slowly released it. She opened her eyes and then rushed to prepare his favorite *fatayer*. She piled the *fatayer* on a plate, putting a colored paper napkin over them and placing her letter on top. She came out of the kitchen and walked nervously to the stranger's table. He had leaned his forehead against the windowpane and was silently watching the passersby on the street outside. She was upset to see a cigarette between his fingers. She stopped shyly a step away from his table, listening to the clear sound of her heartbeats and breathing rapidly. She glanced stealthily at his shoulder, then turned to the old woman who was sitting a way off as her chest heaved up and down. The old woman smiled at her and nodded her head in encouragement. The waitress held her breath and approached on her tiptoes to put the dish at the edge of the table. Then she quickly ran away between the tables to the old woman. She sat beside her, panting.

"I gave him the letter," she stated loudly, pressing her hands to her chest happily.

The old woman patted the waitress's cheek with motherly tenderness. Some of the other customers had seen what the waitress had done. A man and woman whispered together at a nearby table. A girl at another table secretly wished with all her heart that she were writing such a letter to a man, any man in this world. Another man crossed his legs and said angrily, seemingly to himself, "Are there no letters for anyone else? That's not fair—I'm handsome too." A young man dressed in smart clothes, who was eating with his friend, stood up and called to the waitress, "Miss, please, I'd like two letters: a medium one for my friend and a very sweet one for me."

He sat down, laughing along with some others. Even the old woman and the waitress joined in. As for the stranger, he remained leaning on the windowsill, ignoring what was happening and what was being said around him, without the slightest concern for anyone, or for his *fatayer* or even his cigarette.

The minutes dragged by slowly, heavy on her chest as she impatiently waited for the kiss that she had imagined earlier he would blow her through the air. The minutes started shooting bullets at her mood, and her ears were deaf to the orders of other customers. She gazed at the stranger with tight nerves, hoping he would notice her letter. Then the final minute of this exhausting wait fired a bullet of mercy at her patience, killing it. Something mysterious inside her that she did not recognize made her rise and walk directly to his table in front of the silent, apprehensive eyes of the others. She leaned forward until she could see half of his face.

She saw a pale smile on his lips which were colored from excessive smoking, withered features deserted of their usual healthy color and now a pale blue, semi-closed eyelids looking steadily through the window, as if weary of searching for something which had not yet been created.

His cigarette fell from his fingers and rolled across the table, spreading thick ash which indicated that he had lit it but not had time to smoke it. With fear that she had never tasted previously in all the years of her life, the waitress's hand flew to his shoulder, and she shook him. She gasped in immense horror along with everyone else as his body toppled and crashed to the floor. The women at their tables uttered shrieks of fear, and two of them clapped their hands over their eyes, overwhelmed by bitter tears. Many of the men froze like statues as if their minds had momentarily stopped working, and some of them dashed forward, bumping into chairs and tables to bend over the stranger. "Is there a doctor here?" one of them shouted hysterically.

A man squeezed through those gathered around the silent body. "Get away from him!" he cried. "Get away from him!"

He bent over the stranger's chest and tore open his shirt, then palpated his wrist and neck with trembling fingers. He sighed and muttered in a barely audible voice, "It appears he's had a massive heart attack." He paused then passed his palm over the eyes of the stranger. "He's dead," he added humbly.

People around them burst into tears. One of them banged his fists on his table in pain, trying—it seemed—to scare away the angel of death he could sense roaming, quietly and arrogantly, among the tables of the restaurant. The doctor turned to the waitress and asked, "Do you know his name, my daughter?"

She had no strength to speak and answered him by raising her eyebrows, her eyes stunned and lost. It was as if a heavy mountain sat upon her tongue.

Hands slid beneath the corpse, which was mourned by downcast eyes, and some of the men carried the stranger silently out of the restaurant on their shoulders. Everyone inside went out with them and within seconds, the humble restaurant had become an abandoned place. There was no one left but the waitress and the old woman, who started to collect dishes and cups from the tables even through her suffocating sobs.

The waitress collapsed like a broken branch onto the stranger's chair. She heard the wail of a violin coming from the radio.

A first tear trickled bitterly down her cheek, and she picked up her letter from the table with tired fingers. She opened it up, listening to the restaurant door rattling as the autumn wind lashed against it.

The violin's lament, the howling of the old woman, the clattering of the dishes and cups as they were piled randomly on top of each other, the clangs of the door: all played an absurd music in her ears, and she involuntarily started reading the words of her letter out loud. She imagined through her tears that she was singing the lyrics of her letter with a melodic, rhythmic melancholy, as if the ghost of the stranger was sitting in front of her listening with pleasure to the words. She sang her letter as she did the songs she loved, following the rhythm of that absurd music. Then her soul crawled toward a new discovery and in a shining flash she felt all the songs she loved hit at once like a wave in her head. During this second she imagined that before they were ever sung, these songs had also been love letters to strangers whose names nobody knew. . . . Strangers whose lives resembled their cigarettes: ignition and combustion, then ash and extinction, with a few kisses in between, improvised brightly but very quietly.

She contemplated the specter of the stranger standing next to the door of the restaurant, the story of his life under his arm. She raised her hand slowly to her chest and waved him goodbye as he turned and went away.

"God be with you," she murmured between her salty tears.

2nd April, 2010
"The Happiest Evening in the Life of a Young Waitress"
Taken from the collection *A Damp Cellar for Three Painters*

17 FEAR IN THE MIDDLE OF A VAST FIELD

In the morning, I moved into an old flat on the second floor of a faded building in a remote, semi-deserted neighborhood to the north of the city.

An old man sitting by the main door told me that most of the neighborhood's residents had emigrated or been killed during the war that had taken place here decades before. I was not concerned by his words; the important thing was that I was now away from all the people I knew. From now on, none of them would bother me, which meant I should be able to write my best stories here.

There were several rooms in the old dwelling. I felt that one room was enough for me, so I chose a west-facing one that would not be disturbed by the rising sun—it was only the timid light of sunset that darkened its windows each evening.

I cleaned and tidied until midnight, and when I had finished I sat on the sofa to drink a cup of tea and have a couple of cigarettes.

The only thing left to do was to get rid of my bags. I scaled the bathroom door and flung my body into the storage area above to explore.

A load of dust was stirred up and swirled annoyingly about my face. After it had settled, I looked around at the indistinct clutter under the faint light of the moon coming through a small aperture at the top of the wall.

I noticed an ancient teapot next to my knee, so I picked it up and started dusting it off. All at once, thick smoke poured out of its spout and turned into a genie.

"I am at your service, *Sayyidi*—your wish is my command."

"Hmmm . . . I wish to become a scarecrow in a vast field."

"A strange request, *Sayyidi*, but your wish is granted!"

I found myself in the middle of a vast field, my arms extended out sideways and a straw hat on my head.

I felt happy; how beautiful it was to be scary to others, even if they were only birds.

I stood in the field as the days passed. I was amazed at how many birds there were. It was as if there was no special area in their memory that stored fear—they did not care about my presence at all and kept landing in the field to steal the seeds with their beaks.

"Dad, this scarecrow's useless; let's get rid of it," a young boy shouted to his father, pointing at me. They approached with some other kids.

How mean they were! They pulled me out of the ground and, after sunset, took me to their home on the second floor of an unassuming building where they threw me into the storage area.

I do not know how much time has passed since I have been here—perhaps years, perhaps decades.

Tossed carelessly onto the floor of the storage room, nothing around me except misshapen clutter, thick dust, and an ancient teapot.

30th September, 2014
"Fear in the Middle of a Vast Field"
Taken from the collection *Fear in the Middle of a Vast Field*

Last week, my latest love story with a beautiful girl ended in a bitter disappointment—in exactly the same way as all the other love stories I had had in my life. I became convinced that my only success was in smoking. I did not die of this new emotional disappointment, but the distance between my narrow room and the unassuming pub which used to take me three cigarettes to cross now took half a packet.

I walked quickly through the rain-drenched streets, trying to flee from the ghost of the girl which was coming after me. Cars came near to hitting me but also managed to avoid her ghost, so I was not yet rid of it.

By chance I stopped in front of an art shop. Behind its glass façade was a large painting of a beautiful nude lying on a bed surrounded by, I guessed, one thousand and one roses.

She smiled at me. I walked on a few meters and she called my name from inside her painting.

I went back to her. This woman was not a stranger to my memory; I felt that I had seen her in my childhood, but where and how, I could not remember.

"I love you," she whispered to me, and I felt reassured. I entered the store and bought the painting.

After I had hung it in my room above the bed, I sat and contemplated it as I drank a whole bottle of wine. I threw my drunken body onto the bed. A couple of minutes later, this woman fell with a pair of flowers from her painting onto my bed beside me.

I could not believe it. I gasped as she kissed me. She grabbed my hand and put it on her breast. Sweet music opened the door of my wardrobe and came out of it, rushing over to envelop us as we engaged in warm caresses, long kisses, and colorful desires.

When I woke up at noon the next day, the woman had returned to her painting. I picked up the two blossoms and stood on my bed to return them to the painting as we exchanged smiles.

Thus passed many nights. I woke up late, walked for hours in the streets with my cigarettes, then ran away from the rain to the pub, and after several drinks, returned to my room to throw my body onto my bed. And every night, the woman would fall from her painting onto my bed, music would come out of the wardrobe, and we would spend the rest of the night in our delicious tumult. Whenever I awoke, I would return the flowers to the painting.

Truly, girls in paintings were far more beautiful than girls in real life.

Yesterday evening on the street in the rain I discovered that my cigarettes had run out.

A mysterious fear struck me. Then, suddenly, in the wake of this feeling, all the beautiful women with whom I had shared love stories came together in my memory. I could not bear the sound of their curses on me. I quickly bought a fresh packet of cigarettes and fled to the pub where I drank heavily.

One glass followed another. They entered the pub—my former lovers, one by one, to sit around me at nearby tables, looking at me in anger. How had they got to know each other? Each one was from a different neighborhood, a different city, of varying ages and multiple religions!

Everything in the universe was spinning in front of me as I fled to my room. I arrived and wearily threw my body on the bed. I waited for the lady in the painting to fall on me.

I waited a long time, but she did not fall. It was the first night she had not.

I was confused. *Maybe it's her weekly night off,* I thought to myself.

The night passed in a strange way. I was not sleeping, but nor was I awake; a strange silence on a strange night.

In the morning, Muhannad came into my room. He tried to wake me up; I tried to respond to him but could not. He stared at me then moved away fearfully. He started calling my friends and relatives. Muhannad was being weird, and I did not understand what was going on. I looked at the woman and at that moment, I saw her come quietly out of the painting and start climbing upwards.

17th December, 2014
"End of a Painting"
Taken from the collection *Fear in the Middle of a Vast Field*

Oh, you wretched fools! I am so very tired. I am fatigued, exhausted!

I had to curse you all in less than a minute, was forced to do so despite our old friendship. Screw you all, even you, Qusay! I thought you were smarter than the others.

I am not greeting you idiots. I have friends whose foolishness no one in the universe could tolerate. By God, they are so weird. I do not know how they have not caused me to die of a stroke yet, never mind my many years of friendship with their stupidity.

My friends, sadly, are masses of flesh without minds. First off, let us be honest: without alcohol I do not understand them and they do not understand me. So how can we understand each other now?

Indeed, just as my mom told me long ago, I am wasting my talents and intellect with a bunch of fools.

It is true that we have been drinking wine for three continuous hours at this cheap pub, and we have talked about pretty girls with and without clothes, and it is true that the troublemaker Yousef has rolled us many joints. However, despite all of this, I am still fully sober; you, on the other hand, have unfortunately got so drunk and stoned that your sea of stupidity has turned into an ocean in which I am now drowning, slowly and horribly.

We left the pub just a few minutes ago, leaning on one another, laughing loudly like maniacs, indifferent to everything else in the world.

Then, out of nowhere, a missile lands on us in the darkness of the street, throwing us onto the ground as if we are merely tattered rags amidst a heavy storm of blinding dust.

I lie on the asphalt for a while then force myself to sit up, in spite of my terrible pain. I move with difficulty and blood is trickling down all over my body. I gasp in shock as I glimpse on the ground an arm, severed just below the shoulder and burnt like grilled meat. It seems to be a left arm.

I manage to bend over and pick it up. I lift it up, smoke billowing from it, and wave it at you in the thick dust obscuring our vision.

"Who's lost an arm, guys?" I mumble weakly, waving it about.

With your bodies scattered around me on the asphalt, like dark shadows or primitive ghosts, you start slowly waving back to me, as if you are greeting me through the darkness.

I wave at you and you wave back at me. I wave the severed arm and repeat my question, the severity of my pain rendering my voice faint; then you wave again and the dust cackles mockingly.

I am not greeting you! Oh my goodness—it is my fault, I deserve this.

Why do I only befriend idiots?!

Bloody hell! I am tired of waving this arm at you; it is heavy, and I can only hold it with my right hand.

30th April, 2013

"Film Scene from the War"

Taken from the collection *Half an Hour of Agony*

To all those who live inside me, with love.

I do not like the capital, and this was my last day in it before I finally left for my small distant town, back to my old life.

During the day, I was busy roaming the corridors of the university to get my degree certificate. In the evening, I visited the markets to buy things that are not usually available in the outlying towns, then I packed my bags. We entered the bus station together: me, my bags, the night, and the heavy rain.

I noticed a bus which looked like a pallid old man. It was about to leave so I waved at it to stop. The driver's assistant took my bags to put them in the luggage compartment. As soon as I got on the bus my mood was buffeted by a gloomy song, a song that would not appeal even to a prisoner who had spent decades in solitary confinement. The driver did not respond to my greeting. He was smoking, blowing the smoke around indifferently. His inscrutable face caused suspicion to raise its sails in my soul and voyage within my thoughts. There was something incomprehensible on this bus with its dim lights. I started to walk to the back seat, which I do on all my travels as it suits my temperament. From there, I could see all the passengers but none of them could see me.

As I walked away from the driver and his assistant, I inspected some of the other passengers silently scattered on the seats; my heart beat like a drum at a wedding. The passengers in the front seats were of fairly similar ages—young adults, teenagers, a kid . . . But, my God! Were my eyes deceiving me? Was this an illusion? Someone had stolen my face from photos in the family album taken of me over the years and put them on these bodies!

I stumbled past. On the second half of the bus more passengers sat: a few men, one of them elderly. I studied them as suspicion howled inside me like a choking wolf. I stealthily looked at their faces and, despite the darkness, noticed similarities between theirs and my own, as if their faces had been stolen from photos of my future self in my future albums.

I threw my body wearily onto the back seat and the bus set off to leave the capital. I wondered anxiously what damn luck had led me on my last night in the capital to this ill-fated bus? I found no answer in my skull to relieve my soul of this hideous mystery.

As the dismal songs played on, I watched the vile passengers from behind, their silent bodies like crows in a poorly lit museum. I was finding it difficult to breathe. The driver watched me in his rear-view mirror with cynical eyes.

My fate seemed to have been an accomplice to that mysterious driver, for they had both arranged for me an exhausting journey with all the scummy characters that I had lived and was yet to live on a rainy night on the roads between sleeping cities.

The assistant walked among us. Only his voice could be heard on this bus as he distributed some water and repeatedly conveyed to us the tips and warnings of the driver.

Through the glass, I noticed where we were going. "This isn't the way to my town!" I cried.

For years I had traveled home every month; I knew the way to my hometown as well as the features of my face. Despite my weariness and the mountain of fear that had risen above my soul, I stood up to move along the dark aisle between the scumbags to reach the driver. I pressed the button on the tape recorder, making the depressing song stop, and grabbed his shoulder, shaking it fearfully.

"Where are you taking us? This isn't the way to my hometown."

"Shut up. I'm the one who decides the way, and the song too."

He pushed me and I fell next to the door of the bus. He monkeyed with the tape recorder to bring his gloomy song back to life.

The assistant helped me up and took me back to my seat. The eyes of the despicable passengers gleamed with great hatred. It seemed that my attack on the driver had annoyed them.

My breath was rattling, there at the back of the bus on this fucking trip, when a stone came flying, smashing the glass then hitting my forehead; had someone tossed it from outside? I did not know who it was! As I wiped the blood off my face, I realized something fearfully. "I think this stone came from my childhood," I whispered, remembering that when I was young I used to throw stones at buses and run away.

If only someone would save me from this ugly bus.

The glass was scattered on my lap and the cold air, loaded with drizzle, blew into my hair.

The assistant shouted from the front of the bus, "We're taking a break, you can get off for a little while, don't be late back."

I dragged my legs like a soldier coming back from a battle whose cause he had not understood, with deep wounds and mysterious defeat. I got off the bus. None of the other wretched passengers did, as if I were the only one who wanted a little rest. I grabbed a cup of tea and lit a cigarette. The vapour from the tea mixed with the cigarette smoke in front of my eyes, in the rain, as I gazed at those bastards on the bus.

This break, even if rushed, was the right time to think about ending all of this ugliness. I felt like I now had a rare opportunity to end everything vile in my life. I decided to blow up the bus with all its despicable passengers whom I used to be and whom I was to become, so that we would all be done with together. This trip was no longer an ominous fate; it was now a golden opportunity to seize. I sneaked behind the bus, crammed my body underneath, and messed with some of the wires connected to the fuel tank in a way that would make the bus explode a few minutes after it started moving.

As I got back on board, I gazed indifferently at the driver, and he gazed indifferently back. With each step up the aisle I glanced casually at the scumbags; they looked back at me, understanding nothing.

I sat on the back seat and the bus set off. I lit a cigarette and the assistant dashed toward me to tell me that smoking was prohibited. I pushed him and he fell away. Everyone except the driver turned to face us. I stood up, took a deep drag on my cigarette, and screamed in smoke-tainted words, 'Goodbye, scumbags!"

The bus blew up in a massive explosion and our burning bodies inside were all mixed together then scattered randomly among the debris on the road.

Like a slow-footed tortoise, my soul left my body among the dead. Before my eyes closed for the final time, I glimpsed him clearly.

He got up from among us, shaking his clothes off carelessly. Picking his rear-view mirror up from the wreckage, the driver walked away from our bodies, looking up and down the road for another bus to drive.

Reyhanli, 30th January, 2016
"A Bus Full of Scumbags"
Taken from the collection *Help us Get Rid of Poets*

For several months, those of us who were still alive here had been trapped in the rubble of our homes, wearily waiting for the military packs to pounce and slaughter us as they had the residents of the other neighborhoods.

We spent our days yawning inside a huge basement, trying to avoid the shells, thinking in the dark about how our nation would soon be wiped out, and how we would become a mere teaching point on the curricula of other nations.

We imagined that before long there would be no one left in this country apart from members of the military.

It was a Wednesday when a wonderful idea occurred to me: a Great Plan. I gasped and my body shivered as if an *Āyah* had dropped onto me from heaven. My Great Plan—a miracle of the mind, no less—would protect my people from annihilation and extinction; it would give us a unique opportunity for eternal existence in this universe.

When the men came back in the morning from hunting the alley cats whose meat had become our only sustenance, I gathered them together along with the women and children.

"I've decided that I'm going to send a barrel containing a boy and girl from our neighborhood into outer space," I told them with confidence. "It'll land on some planet and new life will begin there, so even if we become extinct here on Earth, in a few centuries we'll be an entire, well-established nation on that other planet."

Some of the people were amazed by my Great Plan while others accused me of madness. My brother and Suaad were the first to endorse it.

Before the war, my brother had specialized in dismantling and repairing engines; since the start of the war, he had been designing explosives. I asked him to make four rockets that could fire a barrel into outer space without being detected by the anti-aircraft devices of our vile enemies.

I found a barrel in the back alley, rolled it along to the basement door and began to clean it up, preparing it for my Great Plan. Next, I conducted interviews with the children in the basement, despite the pleas of some mothers, and finally settled on Yaman and Jumana (both six) because they were the smartest and best looking of all the children. By doing this I was guaranteeing the emergence of a new pure and distinct nation.

Khaldoon, the asshole, came over three times to make fun of me; that bastard didn't believe in my plan, but I didn't care.

I continued to prepare and equip my barrel, a tremendous spiritual euphoria possessing me, while the number of believers in my plan increased hour by hour. My barrel would be another manifestation of Noah's Ark.

Yaman would be the new Adam and Jumana the new Eve on that other planet.

I felt that I was something like a god . . . Not quite a god, but almost a god.

Also, I intended to put several vital things in the barrel, which were as follows:

1. My stories: to be the starting point of popular literature for my new nation on that planet—similar to *The Iliad* for the Greeks and *The Hanging Poems* for the Arabs.
2. Suaad's drawings: to be the foundation of art there.
3. A letter: to explain to the generations that would descend from Yaman and Jumana how their ancestors had been wiped out on planet Earth because of the military massacres.
4. A handful of jasmine: to be cultivated by Jumana on the new planet that would in a few centuries be our new capital.

5. Several personal photos of me: to let the people of my new nation know who had created them.

I leaned over to Yaman. "You might find yourself on a planet with strange aliens," I warned him. "Don't be afraid of them, though; give them the letter and some of my stories and tell them about us and our tragedy."

The following Wednesday the barrel was ready, and the rockets were installed underneath. I yelled at Yaman and Jumana to get inside and crouch down.

I moved away a little to contemplate my barrel, imagining the future generations of my new nation on their new planet, prostrating themselves to statues carved in my likeness with the help of my photos, glorifying the man who had made them.

Suddenly, I heard Jumana crying. I rushed over to the barrel. "My dear! Why are you crying?" I asked her.

She raised her head and pointed fearfully at Yaman. "He kissed me!" she said quietly.

"Oh, that little shit!"

I grabbed Yaman by the hair and pulled him out of the barrel. I dragged him away, slapped his face hard then held him by the ear.

"Listen," I told him. "After landing on the planet do not approach or touch Jumana! Count the days on your fingers and only after twelve years will you have the right to approach her and give her a kiss. If she wishes to kiss you during that time, then that's fine, but you are forbidden. Understand?"

His eyes overflowed with tears. "Twelve years!" he said. "God almighty, that's such a long time!"

"Shut up and stop complaining. You must behave like Adam, not . . . that singer, Alaa Zalzali!"

I dragged him back to the barrel, kicked him inside and threw a bag of essentials on top of him.

I went down to the basement and shouted at everyone to come up and gather around.

They waved sadly to Jumana, who waved back. Yaman did not wave at anyone, but my handprint painted on his cheek vibrated as if bidding farewell to me. I closed the lid of the barrel tightly.

I ignited the rockets and moved away a bit. The barrel took off and flew upward. We kept watching it until it had disappeared into the morning sky.

People looked at me with joy; one of them began clapping slowly, then they all joined in with thunderous applause. Some of them wept, others hugged me.

My Great Plan had succeeded! Yes, we would never go extinct in spite of the massacres; we had won eternity on another planet. I was greater than Noah and my barrel was greater than his ark.

I barely heard their applause; instead, I could hear quiet piano melodies coming from an unknown location.

Suaad was on the verge of running to embrace me in front of everyone— this would have been a declaration ending the secret phase of our love story. I raised my hand to salute everyone and . . .

The barrel landed on my head, smashing my skull and breaking my bones, and I was knocked out.

Some of the young men carried me to the little field hospital where I lay in a coma for three weeks before finally dying. I was buried in the alley behind the basement, next to Jumana's small grave.

I thought I was almost a god but discovered that I was just a fool, and that extinction would be our inevitable destiny. Everyone returned to their boredom and yawning, awaiting the slaughter.

Before I died, I awoke a little from my coma and they told me about Yaman.

After the barrel landed and rolled along the ground, they rushed to open the lid. Jumana was dead. Yaman was only injured, but after coming out of the barrel, and despite the passing time, he continued to believe that his family and everyone else in the basement were extra-terrestrials. He kept telling them about us and our tragedy, then he would try to give them the letter and some of my blood-stained stories. At night he would walk away, sit alone, contemplate his hand, and raise a finger to count. He would shake his head and babble sadly in a faint voice: "Twelve years! God almighty, that's such a long time!"

1st December, 2013
"The Great Plan"
Taken from the collection *The Last Friend of a Beautiful Woman*

My name is Yousef and I am a very ordinary young man. You may pass by me in the marketplace or on the street and never even notice.

I was arrested due to the general turmoil in the whole country. Even though I love the government—goodness knows why—they still arrested me.

I met him in the prison cell. We were from two different cities. He had a charming personality and spirit and was indescribably, beautifully charismatic. I do not think I had ever seen anyone so beautiful in my entire life. I understood from the other prisoners that he had posed a serious threat to the government and had been hard to bring in. He had a million reasons to hate all countries.

They would torture him every night, more than the rest of the prisoners, and when they finally threw him back in the cell, he would make fun of them, making us laugh despite his pain. I loved him so much.

Once when I was overwhelmed by fear he told me, "Don't worry; this dirty government will step down one day. We'll get out of here and fool around with women, tormenting their hearts with our charm and flattery."

His sweet laughter resembled an infant whose lovely mischievousness awakens at each dawn.

On his last night, they brutally tortured him and threw him back to us. He was bleeding all over his body. I bent over him and in pain he whispered to me, "If you ever get out of here, please call my older brother and give him my regards. Tell him I'm sorry for letting him down. I didn't help him enough running our father's shop. I used to wake up late and was always fooling around with women, dragging him into embarrassing situations. He always had too much to put up with from me, but at the end of each month he would share the shop's profits with me as if I'd been working just like him. I planned to name my son after him if I ever got married, but I've failed him even in this."

The silent tears on my cheeks were a mirror in which he saw the beauty of his own face for the last time.

He died. I could not bear it. The most beautiful soul had died in a hideous prison cell. The one who made us laugh from the bottom of our hearts had gathered his wounds and left. I lost my mind. I became delirious, hallucinating. "Marwan, don't die, Marwan, please."

I took hold of his face and raised it up. I let out a great, long, and insane cry as I pressed our faces together.

His blood mixed with my tears to become a *rebab* melody playing desolately in the narrow cell. My cry was a whirlwind that stormed around our tightly glued faces. That night all the prisoners in the other cells heard it.

They wrenched his face away from mine with difficulty and took his corpse from me.

A few days later, they set me free and I went to the bus station. I did not take the bus heading to my city but instead boarded one going to the city of the older brother of that beautiful dead man.

I arrived in the evening. I knew the address of the shop; I walked there and when I arrived, I went inside.

The older brother saw me and hurried happily from behind his desk to hug me warmly.

"I'm sorry, I've always let you down."

"Don't worry about that; what matters is that you came back to us safe and sound."

I am a handsome young man. If you ever happen to catch sight of me by chance on the street or in the marketplace, you will gasp and look at me for a long time. My name is Marwan.

Reyhanli, 18th August, 2016
"When One Face Merged into Another"
Taken from the collection *Help Us Get Rid of Poets*

He rummaged through the first and second drawers then kneeled down to open the third. His father had left for work a few minutes ago and his mother was still in the kitchen making him a *labneh* wrap. Seizing this opportunity, young Rami had swiftly entered his parents' bedroom to search for their large box of chocolates.

He did not know where his mother was hiding it. In the third drawer he found an unfamiliar box; it looked like it could contain chocolate so he opened it hopefully. He gasped as he saw several condoms there. Rami smiled and picked one up to examine it closely.

"Gosh, how cool this is! When did Daddy get a box of balloons? Why didn't Mommy give one to me?"

He decided to take one. Hearing his mother calling him, he quickly closed the box and then the drawer. In the kitchen he took the wrap from his mother and, without her noticing, put it along with his balloon into his bag between his books and jotters. Then he hurried off to school to enter the Year 1 classroom with his little schoolmates.

The bell rang, announcing the end of the first lesson. The teacher and pupils went outside for break. Rami picked up his bag and took out the balloon.

"Look," he said to Sami, who was sitting next to him on the same seat. "Daddy brought me a balloon from the Netherlands. We have relatives in the Netherlands."

Sami stared at the strange balloon, smiled, and said, "Wow, what a cool balloon! But it's a funny shape."

"Because it's original—it's Dutch made."

They took turns trying to blow it up so they could play with it, but after several failed attempts their faces turned red, and it remained uninflated.

Amira approached them and asked curiously, "What's that?"

"It's a balloon from the Netherlands," Rami answered. "But it's very original. We can't blow it up—it needs a pump."

He stared at his balloon with disappointment. Amira took it and tried to blow it up. After several attempts she was able to inflate it a little, and Rami hurried to tie it off with a thread. They laughed happily. Finally they had managed to inflate the balloon, even if just a little, and they started tossing it rowdily to one another between the desks.

Their teacher, Ms. Suaad, entered the classroom and saw them. She was about to move on when the strange object between Rami's hands caught her eye.

"What's that?" she asked him in surprise.

"It's a balloon. My daddy brought it for me from the Netherlands."

Ms. Suaad pursed her lips as she approached to look more closely at this strange balloon, then she gasped, horrified, and pulled back in shock. It was as if she had seen a dead rat in Rami's hands. She fell to her knees and crawled on all fours to the door of the classroom, her body shaking violently. She stood up and screamed at Rami furiously, "Follow me to the office, you nasty boy!"

Then she hurried off as if being pursued by a horrifying ghost.

The children were very surprised by her behavior. Rami did not understand what was going on with Ms. Suaad—it was just a balloon. He walked out of the classroom, heading to the office. On his way in, he passed by a large portrait of the country's leader dressed in his military uniform and looking severe.

As soon as he entered with the balloon in his hands, all the teachers leaped up from their seats. Ms. Suaad had just told them about it. They ran fearfully behind the headmistress's desk and stood behind her chair, covering their eyes. The strange behavior of the teachers was driving Rami mad.

"Stop!" the head shouted at him. "Don't come any closer! I swear I'll slaughter you."

"It's a balloon. An original balloon!"

"A balloon!" one of them muttered angrily. "You son of a . . ."

They all stared at the balloon, terror paralyzing their features; they huddled together as if the balloon were a monster intent upon devouring them.

"Throw it in that bin!" shouted Ms. Maysoon.

The headmistress turned to her, eyes popping in disbelief. "You want him to throw that horrible thing in my bin?" she cried. "And at the end of the day, Abu Amer comes in to take the rubbish out and finds it, which raises his suspicions about me? Then he writes a report to the comrades in the high command about this disgusting thing and they sack me and I'm ruined. No!

"Listen, you rascal; take that nasty thing to Ms. Maysoon's classroom and throw it in the bin there."

Ms. Maysoon turned to the head. "I beg you, madam, don't harm my reputation," she cried. "I swear I didn't mean to offend you."

The headmistress exhaled in exasperation. During their heated argument, Rami had started to cry. "It's a balloon!" he sobbed. "It's a balloon!"

"How will we get rid of it?" the headmistress wondered aloud. It was as if all the worries of the world were resting on her shoulders.

"Let him go outside and throw it in the bin on the pavement by the entrance to the school," Ms. Hadia replied.

The head was on the verge of agreeing with this suggestion when Ms. Samar whispered to them in warning, "When the council workers come to empty the bins tonight, they'll find this thing next to our school. They'll write a report about it to the comrades in the high command, then all our reputations will be ruined."

The head groaned and slapped her forehead, trying to think of a way to get her school out of this bloody disaster without any scandal.

"It's a balloon! It's a balloon!"

"Take the filthy thing out to the garden," shouted Ms. Safiya. "Dig a hole and bury it."

Everyone nodded at this idea, but in floods of tears Rami told them, "After the rain a tree will grow there, and it'll have lots of balloons like this on its branches." He was stammering in his innocent childlike imagination.

For a moment they believed his words, such was the intensity of their fear of this balloon.

"It's possible that one of the other children could dig it up, and then this calamity would be back with us," Ms. Asmaa told them.

Everyone sighed. By this point they were all convinced that their lives at the school were destined for a terrible end.

"It's a balloon! It's a balloon!"

They were still surreptitiously looking at the balloon out of the corners of their eyes, all except Ms. Hind, the only unmarried one among them; she was looking at the balloon with less fear and more curiosity. Ms. Daad noticed and berated her inwardly.

"How did you manage to blow it up?" Ms. Yusra asked him.

"I couldn't. Amira did it."

"What?"

"Amira put it in her mouth and blew it up!"

Everyone started slapping their cheeks as if at a funeral, which caused Rami to bawl all the louder.

"It's a balloon! It's a balloon!"

The headmistress stood up and they stopped, their cheeks red.

"Go outside behind the office and collect some leaves from the ground," she told Rami. "Put this vile thing in amongst them and set it on fire."

She picked up a matchbox from her desk and threw it at him.

"It's a balloon!" Rami was sobbing. "It's a balloon!"

He bent over to pick the matchbox up from the floor, tears streaming from his eyes.

He turned and walked away. On his way out, he happened to look up at the leader's face in his big portrait next to the door. He approached him innocently and stretched out his hand holding the balloon.

"Look, sir, it's a balloon," he told him sadly, hopeful that perhaps at least he would understand and believe him. "It's a balloon." But instead, with horror all over his face distorting the colors of his image, the leader upped and fled from his frame.

Behind the office, Rami kneeled down in front of some leaves. He gathered them together and amassed them around the balloon. He tried several matches before he succeeded in igniting one.

The headmistress and teachers had piled up on top of each other behind the window to watch the burning of the balloon so that their souls could rest easy.

He inserted the lit match between the leaves. He crouched there watching the flames as they rose and grew, quietly staring at them with his head tilted. He imagined the fire becoming ever higher and spreading to burn the office, followed by the school, then the city, and then the whole country.

In his imagination, the fire incinerated everything, except for one thing: him; Rami himself, he who had started it.

His sobs subsided and he smiled.

10th February, 2015
"A Balloon at School"
Taken from the collection *The Last Friend of a Beautiful Woman*

Thick, years-old dust lay heaped on the floor destined to be its final resting place. The smell of mold drifted through the air and the walls had never seen sunlight. In the middle of this cellar, which lay underground like a dead body buried centuries ago, was a poorly made wooden table upon which lay some boxes of color, an old teapot, and a few dirty cups.

To the side stood three easels, each holding a canvas, and in front of these were scattered some chairs.

In the darkest corner a tap shed its tears slowly and quietly, and to the left of this sat a cheap gas stove.

The odor of mold amused itself freely in the darkness of the cellar, weaving about like a dancer in time to the rusty tap's dripping tears.

A pale mouse slithered out of a hole under the tap and wearily wiped from its face a drop of water that had greeted its features.

He spent a few moments observing the place; somehow his mood was not reassured by the smell of the cellar or its suspicious darkness.

The heavy nighttime rain pouring down on the streets outside had prevented the mouse from continuing his journey so he had decided, against his better judgement, to spend the night in the first deserted and safe place he found.

"Where am I now?" the mouse wondered to himself. He felt lonely and thought remorsefully about how it had been a mistake that evening to emigrate from his hometown, the small valley where people's refuse had been dumped for years, bordering the northern boundary of the city.

He had ventured out and foolishly entered the city that evening, the aspiration for a more fulfilling life playing like music inside his skull. But after only a few weeks he was yearning for his place of birth. He had therefore decided to return, but the rain had forced him to take refuge in this strange cellar for now.

The mouse cautiously explored the place then stopped in front of the painted canvases.

A dim and timid light from a lamp outside floated gently through the bars of the window at the top of the wall that overlooked the pavement of a deserted street.

The light slanted across the paintings, rescuing them from the darkness that had the rest of the cellar held in its grip.

Holding his breath, the mouse approached the first canvas, peering up at the picture with difficulty. He beheld a striking girl sitting inside a refrigerator, naked. She hugged her knees to her chest like a frightened child.

The mouse's mouth fell open in surprise. After a few moments he asked, "Why are you sitting in that cold cramped place?"

Tears flowed down the girl's cheeks. She wept quietly and muttered in a suffocated voice, "It's not my fault. That painter heartlessly painted me inside a fridge. If only he'd painted me in a garden or on a balcony. I'll never forgive him! I've been like this for weeks. The cold surrounds me but I don't die. Please, save me—draw a fire next to me, please."

Her gentle pleas and her tears squeezed the mouse's heart. His cells tremored with sadness.

"But . . . I'm no good at drawing," he whispered to her weakly.

"So I'll live for cold centuries in the fridge; neither will death save me, nor do the colors of warmth penetrate the canvas of this prison."

The mouse sighed to the rhythm of her sobbing, the weeping of the tap in the corner and the rainfall outside. He walked on with his head down, looking at the floor, whispering miserably to himself, "Centuries of cold! There's nothing worse than that fate."

He reached the second painting and looked up at it. He could not believe his eyes. He examined it from the front then from the left and finally from the right. Astonishment paralyzed his tongue for a few moments, then he exclaimed, "This is the first time in my life that I've seen a candle with an ear on it, but no flame! What mouse would ever believe I saw a candle with an ear? When did you resign from your original job, Candle?"

"Since some weirdo decided to become a painter," the candle answered angrily. She spat and added, "I'm not a police officer, or a chatty woman's friend. Why this ear? I don't get it."

The candle started hurling terrible insults at the painter and the mouse turned and walked on, careful not to stir up the thick dust on the floor.

In front of the third painting, he gasped with dismay and chills of fear ran through his limbs.

He swallowed as he approached the man with tattered clothes who was hazily depicted in this painting. The mouse gazed sadly at the body writhing in pain as the man held in his right hand his left arm, which had been amputated at the shoulder. A long trail of blood flowed from his shoulder to the bottom of the painting.

"Which war are you from?" the mouse shouted to him.

"I found myself in this form without a war," the man said in a voice that exuded pain. "I didn't commit any sin to make that murderer draw me with an amputated arm. He rejoices in my suffering. I hope God cuts off the hand he used to draw me and inflict all this pain on my body. Please help me," the man begged the mouse, then he let out a deep cry. The mouse did not move closer to the blurry man's painting for fear that he might stumble and drown in the lake of blood at the bottom of the canvas, a lake abundantly supplied by the bleeding of the amputee.

"I don't want to bleed forever," the man repeated hysterically.

The mouse could not think of any solution that would save this man from his eternal bleeding. Annoyed at his inability to save the girl or the man, he fled their pleas to the corner to wet his lips with the water dripping steadily from the rusty tap.

He sat exhausted. Listening carefully, he could hear the echo of the dust's cackles in the corners of the cellar. "Forever, the girl will remain in the refrigerator, neither dead nor alive, immersed in the cold," he muttered sadly as his fearful heart raced. "Forever, the candle will remain without light, with her original characteristics stolen from her. Forever, the man will remain haemorrhaging and in pain with no beginning or end."

He felt utterly worn out as he chanted his last words over and over like a lunatic. His mind was ruthlessly besieged by the girl's tears, the candle's curses, and the pain of the man, accompanied by the beat of water dripping from the tap and the rainfall on the asphalt.

The screams of the girl, the candle, and the man turned into three fists squeezing his heart like an orange. The noise was draining, and his pounding head sank onto the dust. He closed his eyes and groaned then fell into a deep sleep.

A long time passed, and silence reigned over the cellar, then a loud noise woke the mouse and he yawned. He glimpsed the door as it swung open with a massive bang. He scurried under the table in fright.

Three sullen-faced men walked into the cellar. Wordlessly, each of them hung his coat on one of the nails scattered across the walls then sat silently on their respective chairs in front of the paintings, as if they did not even know each other.

After a few minutes which felt like years to the mouse peeking up at them, the first man spoke to his two friends without turning to them.

"I don't know why you draw," he said in a tone which made clear his apathy toward their presence. "After this painting of mine, it's shameful to draw anything! My painting is the last of the masterpieces."

He laughed loudly, putting his index finger up his nose, and added, "Go to the market and sell vegetables. That would be better for you than wasting time doing such ridiculous paintings!"

He stayed silent for a while then said through the cold features of his face, "You're both talentless. My painting is the most beautiful." Biting on his lower lip, he looked carefully at the portrait of the girl and in a hoarse but confident voice whispered, "I'm nearly finished. I just need to draw a deep hole around the refrigerator. At some point the electricity might be cut off or it might break down. No one knows what'll happen in the future. Thus, the girl will remain captive in the hole forever. I'll bury the whiteness of her naked body in the depths of earth. My God! The history of paintings has never before given birth to a work like mine."

He grinned maliciously, displaying his decaying teeth, then picked up a small wooden palette from the table and started to mix his colors enthusiastically. Under the table a tear trickled down the mouse's cheek.

The other two men were completely indifferent to his words. When he had stopped talking, the second spoke, contemplating his own painting happily. "I wasn't expecting to see you today, remember? We said goodbye warmly yesterday. This morning I passed by the vegetable market and thought I'd see you behind a cart shouting about your produce, flogging it to passersby."

He cackled and without turning to the first man added, "Didn't you see my painting yesterday? Sorry, but I'd advise you to look at my splendid picture very closely. After that your fingers won't dare to touch a brush again for the rest of your life."

He laughed again as he wiped away the mucus that flowed out of his nose with the palm of his hand. Then he frowned and went on, "I'm about to finish this. I just need to draw a belt around the candle's waist and attach a knife to it. This canvas will announce to all of humanity that I am the godfather of painting."

He stopped talking, and with an aggressive smile he too started mixing paints on his wooden palette.

A second tear followed its sister down the mouse's cheek as he sat far from their eyes under the table.

The first man seemed about to make fun of the second, but then the third man shouted at them, also without turning away from his painting "I'd advise you both to open a restaurant. Restaurants these days are more profitable than selling vegetables from carts. You remind me of this unsuccessful painter I knew. One day he realized he had no talent, so he stopped drawing and opened a restaurant, and now he's a very wealthy man."

He coughed, spraying his canvas with drops of saliva, and added, "Don't waste your lives making silly paintings."

He stopped talking as he wiped his sputum off his painting. "Anyway," he added as if remembering something important. "I'll bring you some useful information about restaurants tomorrow. Despite your lack of talent, you're still my friends, and I must help you to free art from raiders. My colors and I are soldiers who guard art against restaurant staff."

As he laughed violently, the first man spoke. "Who's that talking?" he asked in fake astonishment. "His voice isn't familiar to my ear."

"It's our friend, the philosopher, of course!" the second man answered in surprise.

"Yes, a philosopher, undeterred by either of you," the third man muttered in a calm and deep tone, as if his voice was coming from an unfathomable cave. "This painting of mine only needs a couple of grams of philosophy, then it'll be ready for eternity."

He swallowed and picked up his brush. With one eye closed and the other half-open, he stroked his thick beard and whispered to himself, "The top layers always resemble the lower ones, but in an inverse way. That's why I have to cut off his left leg. Where are my colors?"

He took his little wooden palette and started mixing the colors that would help him in the amputation process.

The orange nestled between the mouse's ribs under his left lung was completely crushed as he imagined the fate of the man with the missing arm.

The sounds that were coming out of the paintings in the form of cries for help were making him panic, paralyzing his brain.

Looking greedily at their canvases the three painters busily mixed their colors, like someone sharpening his knife to slaughter a sheep.

"Whose turn it is to make tea this evening?" the first man cried.

"I did it yesterday. It's his turn today," the third man replied angrily, pointing at his neighbor.

The second man was indignant and stood up sluggishly in front of the candle with her ear, secretly cursing his fate and his friends. He filled the pot from the tap and returned quickly, carrying the small gas stove which he placed beside the table. He added loose tea and sugar to the water then put the pot on the stove.

He went back to sit on his chair, breathing heavily, and waited impatiently for the water to boil as he looked fondly at his painting.

Under the table the mouse's agitation increased as he attempted to escape the noise made by those voices.

The stifled weeping of the girl in the fridge, mixed with the curses of the candle as she prepared herself for her final destiny, mingling with the reverberating "*No!*" of the amputee.

The mouse squealed weakly, wishing he had never escaped from the rain into this cemetery that was being built by the colors of the three painters with their sullen faces. He would have reached his country located in the valley of rubbish to the north of the city by now.

The mouse came out from under the table and the groans and curses and echoing "*No*" slapped him in the face. He cried out again as he watched the three painters sharpening their colors. He shouted at them one last time, but they did not notice him.

He dashed forward and climbed the leg of the table; he walked across the top to the corner and stood next to a matchbox.

He craned his neck to look down over the edge and his face was hit by steam through which he managed to spot the tea boiling in the pot.

"Please," the girl in the refrigerator whispered sadly to him.

"I beg you," the amputee beseeched him miserably.

"Help me," the candle called out to him.

The mouse jumped, not hesitating or giving his mind a chance to reconsider for even a second. He jumped off the table to fall into the teapot boiling on the gas stove, and his body plunged into the hot liquid.

As he hit it, drops of dark tea splashed out around the pot.

The street lamp outside weakly illuminated a small part of the damp cellar space.

In harmony with the dim lighting, they finished mixing the colors on their palettes.

Three cigarettes were simultaneously lit and greedily dragged upon by dry lips.

The stillness as they contemplated their paintings with eyes ready to shoot colors at the canvases was only disturbed by the sound of water dripping from the rusty tap, the raindrops falling from the clouds of the night, and the trembling of the teapot when its contents had started boiling a few moments earlier.

The second man stood up, grumbling. He placed the lid on the pot and brought it over to the table.

"Not now, give it a minute," the third man demanded. "Wait until the tea's properly infused."

The second man exhaled angrily. He fetched the cups then calmly swilled the tea in the pot before lifting it high to pour the liquid into them. He took one cup then with disgust gave the other two to his friends.

None of them uttered a word. Each took a deep drag on his cigarette and sipped his tea. They looked at their paintings and compared them with what they had drawn in their imaginations.

They drank silently, their eyes like snakes', dripping poison.

The first man came to a decision and lifted his brush to the face of his painting, but the brush did not make it to the canvas. Instead, its owner toppled over and fell from his chair onto the floor with his cigarette. His body writhed a little then stopped moving.

The second man ignored him until he had swallowed the last sip of his tea. He stood up, irritated by the behavior of his friend which had spoiled his mood. He leaned over him before also collapsing; his breath rattled for a few seconds then silence reigned again.

The third man smiled and did not pay them any attention. He sipped the remaining tea in his cup and put his brush on the thigh of the man with the amputated arm. Then he felt severe dizziness in his head and fell, his body rolling onto the floor next to the other two, also silent and pale.

Three bodies, three cigarette butts, three brushes, the things scattered next to the table, in a dim spotlight coming from the streetlamp through a window at the top of the wall.

The dust, which had been angered and stirred up during their falls, slowly landed on their clothes, faces, and bulging eyes.

A gust of cold air blew through the half-open door, catching her painting and making it fall to the ground. She groaned for a few moments then looked around suspiciously.

The pallor of the faces emboldened her heart, so she got up and ripped the canvas of her painting so she could wrap it around her naked body like a coat.

She tiptoed to the second painting and pulled the candle from her canvas. She gently pulled the ear off then threw it away with revulsion. It flew over to stick on the wall.

The girl jumped softly over the prone, motionless bodies and took a matchstick from the box on the table to light the candle.

The flame of the candle illuminated a wide area of the cellar. The girl took the candle as she shyly approached the third painting. She smiled at the man with childlike joy, but his features were twisted in agony and the smile faded from her face.

She was at a loss for a while, but after a few moments she picked up a brush and one of the palettes from the floor, dipped the brush in some of the paint and drew a new arm on his bleeding shoulder, finally finishing after some time.

He smiled from inside his painting but remained stuck to the canvas.

"Please, get out of the painting," she begged him, but he did not utter a word or make any movement.

Her eyes were seized by a desire to cry, but her heart whispered something to her. She smiled again and leaned forward, moving her face closer to his. She kissed him on his cheek with nervous lips, and his body fell from the canvas.

The dust on the floor stirred up in revolt against him. He waved his hand in front of his face to protect it from its wrath as he coughed. He quickly rose to his feet and hugged her to his chest longingly.

He groaned a little because of the small wound on his thigh but pulled himself together and smiled at the innocence of her angelic face.

His fingers intertwined with the fingers of her right hand. By the light of the candle in her left hand, they cautiously hurried to the door of the cellar, fearful of making any sound that might help these painters awaken from their hibernation.

He quietly opened the door fully. Both of them turned around to look with joy at the bodies thrown randomly on the floor.

He looked into her eyes with love, and she looked back into his. His fingers tenderly embraced hers, then they slipped out of the door with their candle.

After they had fled, the darkness breathed a sigh of relief and returned to devour large areas of the cellar space.

Thick, years-old dust descended to land on the objects which would be its final resting place.

The smell of mold permeated the walls which had not seen sunlight since their creation.

In the darkest corner the rusty tap practiced its eternal hobby of shedding water droplets in a monotonous and regular rhythm.

Now there was nothing in that damp, dark cellar lying underground like a corpse buried centuries ago. Nothing but three bodies silently lying in its vacuum, and three chairs scattered randomly on its floor. All of these things would, from that moment, become a delicious meal for the dust. There was also a poorly made wooden table with some boxes of color and a few dirty cups.

And an ear on the wall and an old teapot with a corpse inside.

Damascus, 29th December, 2008
"A Damp Cellar for Three Painters"
Taken from the collection *A Damp Cellar for Three Painters*

I sat silently for three or four cigarettes, gazing with suspicion through the billowing smoke at my clothes. They were hanging on a wooden rack next to my bedroom door. I had no memory of hanging them up so neatly this afternoon! Surely someone else had been messing with them—my mom? Maybe. I exhaled indifferently then heard her calling me for dinner from the kitchen. My stomach was done with her plain soup night after night, but I thanked her for her kind invitation in a loud voice.

I got off my bed, walked wearily over to the chair and sat at my desk. Several novels were scattered around upon it. I smoked another cigarette but even these had lost their taste. This ennui had ravaged my soul for months; I was on the verge of suffocating. I felt that my soul was being devoured with relish by all the boredom in existence.

I had graduated two years ago from the Faculty of Arts English Department but had yet to find a job. Had it not been for the pension of my deceased father, we—my mother and I—would have starved to death in our gloomy home.

I was ashamed that I couldn't help my mother. I wished I could support her a little to improve the condition of our house and our lives so that this old woman could be happy and relax a little, could forget about dragging me by the ear to the bathroom for a few days. How I hated water! Why, I don't know; I just hated it.

Two years passed. In the mornings I wandered through the city on my bicycle, going between companies, institutions, and private schools searching for a job opportunity; even working as an attendant wouldn't be a problem. In the evenings I entertained myself reading novels.

Then it occurred to me: why didn't I write a novel? A wonderful idea had been floating around inside my head for a while, and I felt that it was now ripe. I was sure it would turn out to be a distinguished novel, especially since there would be no water in it. Even supposing it ended up being just average, at least while I was writing it, I would be protecting my soul from its aimless roaming during those evenings of tedium and boring soup.

Without further hesitation I picked up my pen and started writing in a simple notebook. I was rather surprised by my enthusiasm—I didn't know where it had come from.

It took me three and a half months to finish writing the novel. Each afternoon, following my nap and with the help of coffee and cigarettes, I would start writing and continue late into the night. Throughout these weeks my mom observed me fearfully. I enjoyed the writing a great deal; it gave me so much pleasure I wished it wouldn't end. Writing the words of my novel on the paper brought me untold happiness.

The evening I finished writing, I couldn't actually believe it. How could it be that a failure like me had written a novel? My God! Soon my mind was flying with joy. I leapt into the middle of my room and started singing, dancing around and clapping like a drunk lunatic. It may be true that I'd failed to find a job, but I had written a novel! It seemed that I was destined only for great things.

This was a historic occasion, and we should have been celebrating it. *Where are you, Mom? Your only son has written a novel; you should be ululating and holding your head high.* I rushed to her in the kitchen where she was standing in front of the hob, cooking her miserable soup. I grabbed her by the hand and started dancing with her. It was as if we were lovers in some classic French film. I snatched up a cup of the hot herbal concoction my mother drank to help her tolerate the ailments of old age and raised it up in front of her shouting, "To your health, Mom! A toast to great novels!" I took a sip—good God, how bitter it was—then waved goodbye to her, one hand on my stomach, and returned to my room.

At my desk, I started to arrange the pages of my novel carefully, like it was a beautiful lady whose charms were these pages. I caressed the novel, touching the corners gently . . . then suddenly my thoughts collided with a harsh truth which gradually spread over my face.

I was very familiar with the writers, critics, and journalists of this unfortunate country, and I knew that they would have neither the time nor the inclination to discuss the novel of an obscure young man, no matter how important it was. All their attention was currently focused on female writers and poets—and the shorter her skirt, the greater the number of reviews appearing in newspapers and magazines to highlight the importance of her creative achievements.

I sighed. The sadness in my chest craved a cigarette so I lit one. And then a brilliant idea came to me, one that could save my novel and spare it from death. I remembered years ago reading in a Russian short story about a novelist who, when no one gave a toss about his stories, decided in a moment of madness to have them printed under a foreign name, making them look like literature from some other country and thus ensuring their extraordinary popularity.

I would do the same. My madness was no less than his; the important thing was that my novel survive. I decided to present it to a publishing house as a novel written by a Patrick Jimpson, which I, Esa Zakaria, had translated from English. Such was this idea's appeal that I called a renowned publishing house and booked an appointment with its director.

The next afternoon, I got dressed and tucked under my arm a large yellow envelope containing the manuscript of my novel. Then I rode my bicycle along the streets to the publishers. I told the receptionist that I was the translator Esa Zakaria, and that I had an appointment with Mr. Basem Alaa, well-known critic and director of this place.

When I entered his office, I almost burst out laughing. Mr. Alaa looked just like a walrus sitting behind his desk. I contained my mirth and sat down in front of him to tell him about this novel that I had faithfully translated from the English.

He asked me the name of the writer. "Patrick Jimpson," I replied. He pursed his lips, wiping his bald head with his hand.

"I've never heard of him!" he said, sounding surprised.

As planned, I began my confident explanation:

"He lived in England in the mid-eighteenth century, but his origins go back to Northern Ireland, and he was a supporter of the Irish Republican Army. So in England, they always tried to ignore his narrative experience for national and religious reasons, and—"

"Has the Irish Republican Army existed since the eighteenth century?" he wondered in surprise.

"It's been around since the fourteenth century," I invented. "At that time there was a well-known correspondence between the IRA and the Brethren of Purity in our region. These correspondences are preserved in an archaeological manuscript which is considered an important historical document in the Library of Congress in Washington. They're known as 'The Correspondence of the Brethren of Purity'."

He fiddled with his tie, nodding his head to suggest he knew this information, then asked for the manuscript. I gave it to him.

He looked at the title, flicked through its pages, read a line here and there. He smiled. It seemed it might appeal to him. He put it on his desk where there were already several other manuscripts and said, "We'll get back to you in a month to let you know whether or not we're going to print it. The house committee must have a thorough look at it. Have a nice day, brother Esa."

I understood that this was my cue to leave. I stood up to shake his hand warmly and then left.

The receptionist wrote down my phone number as I stole furtive glances at her ample breasts, imprisoned harshly inside her tight-fitting blouse.

When I got home, I threw my bicycle behind the door then threw my body onto the bed. I exhaled irritably. I was sure that the publishing house committee would not like the novel and would decide not to print it. They would also discover that Patrick Jimpson was not real, but the product of my imagination; then perhaps the IRA would issue a statement condemning my words and deeds. The days passed and these fears and my mom's soup battered my soul and my stomach.

On the seventh day, the phone rang. It was Basem Alaa.

"Good evening, Mr. Zakaria," he said warmly. "The house committee has agreed to print the novel you translated. The committee experts described it as one of the best novels of Western literature. If you don't mind, could you come to my office now to sign the contract and—"

"Now? Sorry, my friend—I have some appointments this evening. I could drop by tomorrow afternoon."

I did not have any appointments, of course. I had made it up in order to satisfy my desire to feel like an important person.

I did not sleep that night but practiced my signature over several dozen white sheets of paper.

I left my bicycle a couple of streets away from the publishing house, afraid that one of the employees there would see it—a bike was hardly suitable for a very important translator like me.

"Coffee, no sugar," I said to the beautiful receptionist as I walked into Basem Alaa's office.

"Sorry I'm late," I said to Basem Alaa as I sat down angrily and lit a cigarette. "It took me a long time to find a parking space. The narrow streets in the city center are so bloody annoying!"

I tried to conceal my laughter as I shook hands with several men in the room. It seemed that they were the company's advisory committee. They all looked like walruses, except one who looked more like a penguin.

I drank my coffee, sitting with my legs crossed, then we signed the contract. I immediately received a good sum of money and we agreed on percentages.

Within two weeks, the novel had been printed and distributed to every bookshop; there were also some advertisements in the press.

Its sales within the first two months made us gasp in surprise—they were far higher than we had estimated. Furthermore, many articles and studies were being written about it and published in several magazines and newspapers.

After another couple of months, a second edition of the novel was printed along with a new contract stipulating higher profits. At the beginning of each week Mr. Basem Alaa would send me the money with his private driver.

The big money made me very happy. I bought my mother everything she needed and myself everything I could have dreamed of: new clothes, shoes, hats, a pipe, nice decorations for my bicycle and pictures of beautiful models and Hollywood stars which I hung around my room.

A few times I managed to cleverly dodge journalists and broadcasters who wanted to interview me about the novel. I was afraid that my lie about Patrick Jimpson would be revealed under a bombardment of questions.

One evening, I had slipped into my new luxurious pajamas and was sitting on the sofa in front of the TV, happily eating nuts, drinking juice, and smoking my pipe. The nuts were wholly delicious and a spiritual euphoria engulfed my whole being while I chomped on them. At that moment, I came to a decision: "I have to translate a second novel by Patrick Jimpson."

My stomach started dancing around inside my body. Suddenly the phone rang; I put the handset carelessly to my ear.

"Hello," said a mysterious voice. "Can I speak to Esa?"

This was the first time since my novel had been printed that a stranger had addressed me by my name on its own, without a 'Mr.'!

"Mr. Zakaria speaking. I apologize, but I'm not giving any press or radio or television interviews, and—"

"We need to meet, my dear Esa."

The disturbing confidence in his voice ruined the flavor of the nuts on my tongue. "Why do you want to meet me?" I asked him in a dry voice.

"Well . . . I am Patrick Jimpson, the author of the novel you translated, and I want my share of the profits."

I gasped, unable to believe the words that were boring into my ear and had made me unintentionally kick the table. "You liar!" I shouted into the phone. "You're not even real—I created you. It's *my* novel, you son of a bitch!"

"I'm coming for you, you bastard. If you're any kind of man, you'll wait for me. I want my share of the profits, whether you like it or not. You're just a translator."

He hung up. My whole body was shaking. Damn this evening. Was it possible for this Patrick to be real? Impossible! He was a lie. *He's coming to you with all of the IRA*, a devil screamed inside my head. I saw my glass, plate, and pipe broken on the floor . . . as if my life itself had fallen off the table to shatter upon the tiles. I went to light a cigarette, trying to calm down, but it fell on the floor too. My heart sank as I heard vile banging on the door of our house accompanied by piercing shouts.

I rushed to the window to peek into the alley. I could just see him in the darkness of the night, kicking the door violently. "Come out here, you idiot!" he screamed. "Where are you, you fraud? Give me my share of the profits! I'm the owner of this novel and you're only a translator."

Lights started to set several windows down the alley aglow. There was a big scandal about to break, threatening to gobble up our bleak house in front of all the others. I went up to the roof, stumbling over my own feet. I leapt across the roofs of the neighbors' houses until I reached a distant alley, then I ran away from the neighborhood and from this nightmare. Fortunately, my mom was off visiting my aunt.

I went to my friend Adham's house.

"The most important translator in the country visits his friends in the middle of the night, barefoot!" he exclaimed in surprise when he opened the door. "Strange."

Damn it, Adham: I'm not a translator.

I used his phone to call my mom. She picked up and asked, "Where are you, son? Your friend Patrick is here. He's waiting for you and wants to give you his second novel to translate. He's very nice and seems to admire you very much. I put him in your room."

Even you, mom, thought that your son was just a translator! It felt like God Himself was going to bring me to account as a translator, not a novelist, on Judgement Day.

I told her that I would be away for a few weeks and promised to send the money she needed every month, then I hung up before she could start debating anything with me.

I only left Adham's house a few times during those weeks. Patrick would run me ragged each time, chasing me from street to street and alley to alley all over Damascus. My God! Where had this creature come from? He was like a ghost pursuing me and setting ambushes in the streets, transforming my life into an unbearable nightmare.

One night, after a long and tiring spell of thinking, I smiled slyly: I had thought of a way to get rid of Patrick permanently at last. "I'll imprison Patrick in this country forever," I whispered to myself, sighing in relief as I helped myself to some wine for the first time since I'd run away from home.

With the help of Adham's uncle who lived in Eastern Europe, I managed to get a passport skillfully counterfeited—the uncle had contacts in those international gangs. It cost me a fortune. The first page of my new European passport showed my handsome face with its charming smile, but it did not bear my name: I had requested that it be made in the name of Patrick Jimpson. One hell of an idea. I did not tell Adham anything. I stared at the passport throughout the evening, laughing manically. I had defeated him.

I booked a flight to London and went to the airport the next morning. I was hoping to see Patrick on the way, setting an ambush for me on some street, so I could bid him a gloating farewell, but he wasn't around. I waved goodbye to my country through the aeroplane window; I waved to my mother sadly and to Patrick with a smirk. "Goodbye, Patrick," I murmured with confidence. "You piece of shit. You're going to be a prisoner in this country forever; you can't leave it twice."

I laughed aloud and the other passengers turned to look at me in surprise as I chattered ecstatically: "You won't be able to leave it twice!"

On board that aeroplane, in the middle of the endless sky, I decided to completely forget about Esa Zakaria. High in the sky, between the clouds, I started to train myself to become Patrick Jimpson.

Good God, how wonderful London fog is! It provokes the appetite of imagination, pushing it up to fly freely to other worlds. Even after two years there, my admiration for London's fog remained endless. It was part of my soul.

When I arrived, I found a simple but decent job. My proficiency in English helped me a great deal. So it was that for two quiet years I washed dishes in a modest restaurant. In the evenings I lay on my bed in a small room above the restaurant and read English novels. At the weekend I walked happily with my endless fantasies through the fog of London, like I was playing a game of hide-and-seek with an imaginary friend. I also enjoyed feeding the swans in the London parks, like any ordinary Englishman.

One day, Mr. Henry, the owner of the restaurant, patted me kindly on the shoulder. Looking happily at the glistening dishes, he said, "You're a good guy, Patrick. England is proud of you."

One fine evening, I waved alongside him and many others to Queen Elizabeth II as she passed in front of us in a luxurious horse-drawn carriage. Michael, my handsome co-dishwasher, pinched my arm and winked at me, saying, "Her Majesty looked at you for a long time, Patrick! It seems she likes you."

We laughed like little children—Mr. Henry, the handsome Michael, young Jack, and me. Officer Mark, the final guard in the Queen's procession, also heard; he did not arrest any of us but smiled silently.

During the summer I had a passionate love affair with sweet Margaret, which was very tiring for my bed. Her father Lord Charles, however, rejected the idea of our engagement; in the opinion of his odd disposition I was not of a noble lineage, my features indicating that I was of Irish origin, and was good for nothing but washing dishes. "My dear Margaret, you're not a dish!" he said angrily to his daughter.

My God, how these words insulted my ego! They were so painful that they imprisoned me in my room for several days as I racked my brains for a way to prove to Lord Charles that I was not as insignificant as he thought.

Then a wonderful idea came to my mind that made all the cells in my body shiver. I said to myself, "Why don't I print my brilliant novel here in London?"

I thought all night and came to a decision at dawn: I would rewrite the book, but this time in English. Since the critics here were very astute, I would not claim that it was written by me, Patrick Jimpson—if they investigated they would discover that I was not of British origin, causing all kinds of trouble. Instead, I would pretend that I was the translator and that the novel had been written by a young man who had committed suicide in Damascus long ago: Esa Zakaria.

So, throughout the nights of the next two and a half months, I wrote my novel again in English. Mr. Henry noticed that the brightness of the dishes had diminished and became upset with me.

Once I had finished writing, I gathered the papers together happily. My soul soared with joy. I went to a famous publishing house in central London. The proprietor, Lord James, welcomed me into his office. I sat in front of him and handed him the manuscript.

"I've translated this novel by a writer from Damascus," I explained to him. "A young man who committed suicide in the eighteenth century and—"

"Were the Arabs familiar with the art of the novel in the eighteenth century?" Lord James interrupted me in amazement.

"Yes, sir," I answered. "There were several rather interesting endeavors, but they were overlooked for religious and political reasons to do with the East and its mentality and temperament."

"No problem, my dear Patrick. I'll look at the novel over the coming month, then I'll give you a call to let you know what I think."

While I had been talking, Lord James's dog had been staring at me in disgust. I was not in the mood for its rough features. I felt as though it knew that my words were all invention. *New discovery: it appears that dogs can recognize lies, just as they can predict earthquakes.* I was fortunate that this big creature did not speak English, otherwise it would surely have exposed me. When Lord James embraced me farewell, I stuck my tongue out tauntingly at the animal over his shoulder.

Four days passed. Mr. Henry could no longer tolerate the decline in the sparkle of the dishes. Just as he was about to start scolding me, Lord James phoned me at the restaurant office.

"My dear Patrick, the novel is very impressive and really amazed me. A great novel that could only have been created by a young soul intent on

committing suicide and leaving this world. Can you come now to my office
o we can sign the contract?"

"Apologies, my friend, but I can't come just now. I've got some dishes
need to—I mean, I have some appointments. We can meet tomorrow
morning."

I ignored the look of surprise on the face of Mr. Henry, who was sitting
behind his desk in front of me. I did not go back to wash the dishes but
instead went up to my room. Michael, however, told him about my project
translating a novel from the East.

A week after we had signed the contract, the novel was issued and
distributed to every bookshop in each of Britain's cities. The profits were
unreal as the book achieved a high sales rate, topping the list of best-selling
fiction. Within a few months, second and third editions were printed and
distributed in other English-speaking countries.

A leading director from Wales called me to discuss his desire to make a
film adaptation of the novel to be released worldwide.

The journalists here were very annoying but I was adept at evading
them; their clever questions were scary and my answers could have exposed
my lie.

I gave Mr. Henry a copy of the novel and embraced him warmly. He had
been like a father to me for more than two years. Michael wept as he bid
me farewell. "Our white dishes will miss your hands so much, Patrick my
friend," he sobbed.

I left the restaurant and rented a beautiful flat in a swanky neighborhood in North London. Its balcony overlooked that magical fog my soul
so adored. I also bought a brand-new car. I wished that I had an agent
to answer Margaret's call, but I had to do it myself. She was insistent on
getting back together. Presumably, news of her ex-boyfriend's fame had
reached her. I made my apologies and turned down her invitation to go

and see her, although I promised that I would visit soon to console her over the death of her father.

One beautiful evening, I had eaten a delicious pasta dish before lighting a luxurious Cuban cigar. I puffed on it and took a sip of my Parisian wine, watching a piece on a leading British TV channel all about me and the novel I had translated. There were photos of me, stealthily captured by those mischief-making journalists, walking the streets or around the shops, and once while I was on my balcony. There followed a quick chat with Lord James and a brief testimonial from Mr. Henry as one of my friends; I was pleased that his speech did not mention my dishwashing history.

I sipped my wine and took a big puff on my cigar, feeling proud. "I'll need to translate a second novel by Esa Zakaria," I whispered tipsily, sinking into my sofa.

The phone rang. To hell with those troublemaking journalists. *I am now in a state of spiritual ecstasy, idiots.* I put the receiver to my ear.

"Hello. Is brother Patrick there?"

"Yes, speaking."

"How are you doing, *Abu Al-Pawatreek*? It's Esa Zakaria, the author of the novel you translated. I want my share of the profits right now. Also, my mother says hi, you sweetest of scoundrels."

I jumped up from the sofa, dropping the wine bottle, glass, and cigar on the floor. My whole being was shaking with terror.

"There *is* no Esa Zakaria! It's just one of my lies, you crook!"

"You're a liar. Wait there—I'm coming for you, Patricko, you little shit."

He hung up.

A great fear screamed loudly inside my heart: Esa was coming.

I got dressed hastily, not even putting on a tie, and rushed out to my car, stumbling over my own feet.

In the rear-view mirror, I caught sight of a young man in the distance, coming closer on a bicycle. He was brandishing a heavy stick, shouting threats and swearwords. Before he could reach me, I started up the car and sped away.

I should have run him over, got rid of him for good under my wheels, but I was afraid of being charged for the murder of a foreign citizen, which could put me behind bars for twenty years.

Lonely nights passed as I lived on the run between London hotels. As soon as I entered a room I had booked I would receive a call from Esa containing a thousand obscene insults and death threats. Whenever I drove my car, he would emerge from a side street on his ridiculous bicycle, brandishing his stick. I spent many sleepless nights driving around in my car, spurred on by terror; my nights were filled by horrifying nightmares in which a thousand and one Esas set about my head with their big sticks as it bled rivers of fear.

On these miserable nights I aged a thousand years; I was slowly dying. My soul could no longer bear the nightmares that would surely have been more than enough for all the people from Damascus to London.

Dear God, help me. I beseech You to save me from this terrible dilemma. I am Your righteous and faithful son, Patrick. For all Your clouds and Your heaven, have mercy upon me, spare me this torment, and save me from the dark scandal which is about to devour me.

The people scattered through the labyrinthine streets of London inclined their heads in grief for my moribund features. Without a tie, I wandered aimlessly every night between the city's taverns.

God did not respond to my prayers in the faded hotel rooms. Alcohol became divine.

Tonight I was drinking heavily while a deep misery downed me as if I were its favorite wine. I was incredibly drunk when the bartender whispered to me that an Esa Zakaria was on the phone regarding an urgent matter. I did not run away this time; something inside me surrendered completely.

The kind barman supported me to stagger to the phone. If only I had stayed at the restaurant, washing the dishes.

"You have no third character to escape to, Patrick," Esa announced to me over the phone. "There's no way out. I'd advise you to meet me so we can negotiate a fair settlement for both of us. What do you think?"

My fatigue, misery and sadness replied as one: "OK. Where and when do you want to meet, Esa?"

"In three hours, at midnight, under London Bridge. Don't bring a weapon. My stick'll kill you even if you have a gun."

He cackled brutally. The same kind barman helped me to my room on the second floor. He was contemplating my face but did not say anything. There was a silent lament for my soul in his eyes.

I felt as if he was saying goodbye to me. Everything was spinning in my head like a violent storm and my soul swung back and forth between terrible agonies like the pendulum of an old clock.

I threw my body onto the bed. I did not know how long I slept; my sense of time had faded completely. It was a restless sleep during which I drowned in a hell of torture. The claws of some strange creature came out of nowhere to maul my soul.

All my pains disappeared the moment I awoke. I looked at the room around me. It was utterly silent, its furniture colorless. The place was engulfed in a terrible stillness.

I noticed the clock: midnight. I remembered the appointment. I ran out of the room and the receptionist did not notice me when I left the key at the front desk. It looked like he was drunk.

I tried to start my car but there was something wrong with it. It was probably also drunk. I tried to hail several taxis but none stopped. Surely they were all drunk too! It seemed to me that the whole universe was drunk tonight.

I had no choice but to walk to London Bridge. Despite the crowded streets, filled with people and cars, I could not hear anything. I walked quietly, without fear, without my car or even a bike.

I reached the bridge half an hour late. Feeling surprisingly calm, I went underneath.

Under the bridge I caught sight of two ghostly figures through the fog, standing by the river. I crouched down to hide among the bushes as I watched them, then stealthily moved closer.

As I got nearer, I gasped in shock: Esa and Patrick were standing face to face right in front of me.

I could not believe it. I looked at them closely. It was indeed Esa and Patrick, complete with all my features. I knew them well—better than any other being; I had seen them countless times in the mirrors of Damascus and London.

My God, how alike they looked! It would be more or less impossible to distinguish between them at first glance.

All of a sudden, their voices rose, their limbs tensed, and pent-up rage permeated their features. Next thing they were hurling hard punches and harsh kicks at each other.

"The novel's mine!" Esa screamed. "I created it! You're just a fucking translator!"

Patrick threw him to the ground and spat on him. "It's my novel!" he retorted furiously. "It's you—you're the fucking translator, you piece of shit!"

I could see that Patrick was a little stronger than Esa, but Esa was none too weak either. *God! They'll kill each other. I've got to help them, put a stop to this bloody fight.* I tried, but it was as if I were a statue.

They fell on top of each other, rolling around in their own blood on the riverbank. Their struggle was becoming ever more brutal. They did not notice me at all, standing watching them, impartial and idiotic.

Nor did they notice the water as it silently drew them into the middle of the river, like two boats that had collided in the fog.

I finally ran frantically to the water's edge and shouted to them. I was desperate to break up the fight, to end their cruel encounter, but unfortunately I could not swim. Indeed, I had centuries-old aquaphobia. The mutual admiration between me and all things in the universe did not extend to water; we did not love each other.

When Esa and Patrick realized that they were in the middle of the river, they forgot their conflict and started thrashing about in the water, screaming like two lost children.

The river water washed the blood from their faces and began to swallow them like a hungry beast, indifferent to their screaming. My grandmother once told me, "Rivers have no language. They don't understand the words that people have invented." I remembered this story well, but could not remember where she had told it to me: Damascus or London?

Only now they were drowning did they see me. They stretched their arms out toward me in horror, their instinct to survive.

"Please, sir, save me," Esa begged in fear. "I am you."

"Sir, I beg you to save me, not him," Patrick pleaded in terror. "You are me."

How I wished I could save at least one of them! How I regretted my inability to swim. It seemed that tonight I was to be good for nothing but observance.

I fell to my knees on the riverbank, weeping bitterly, like a monk defeated by his faith in others. Their struggle with the water was terrible to behold through the fog, like watching the entire universe battling the river.

Soon they were defeated by it.

I waved to them through tears of desolation as I resigned myself to the fate of their deaths.

"Goodbye Esa, goodbye Patrick. I was happy the day I put you on, and I was happy the day I put you on, too."

As they disappeared under the water, I bid farewell to everything inside me. It was the first time I had ever wept and would also be the last. They drowned together; their bodies with limbs intertwined in a sad embrace sank all the way to the bottom of that London river whose belly was now stuffed with two elegant corpses.

There was nothing left of me now except for a bicycle in Damascus and a fancy car in London, which as of tonight would be left to the transcontinental dust, and also a novel that had two writers and two translators in two different countries.

A long time passed; I did not have any way to measure it as I wandered through a still and silent cosmos like a lost soul without a human being to veil its loneliness, invisible, traversing the cities of Europe with the blowing breeze.

Sometimes I cursed Esa, at other times Patrick. During my endless nonexistence I miserably amused myself in train stations and corporate offices, in cafés, bars and restaurants, in schools and homes, approaching coat racks indifferently to ponder cynically the clothes people had hung upon them, messing with them a little, sighing. During these infinite wanderings of my lost soul I avoided, like any nothing, getting too close to the water.

10th April, 2014
"Tale of a Wandering Soul Lost in Europe"
Taken from the collection *The Last Friend of a Beautiful Woman*

It was rare for me to remember my dreams. Often after I awoke, I knew that I had had a dream but I was never able to remember it. Thus my life continued: neither remembering my dreams nor they remembering me. An age-old miscommunication between us.

But this afternoon when I woke up, as I lay in my bed, I remembered the dream I had had down to its smallest detail.

I dreamed that there was a pandemic that had spread all over the planet, killing most of the population. At the same time, sea levels had begun to rise, threatening the lives of those who had survived. Like Noah, I set about building an ark for whatever could be saved from among the various forms of life on Earth. When I had finished, I chose a pair from each species of animal to come aboard. I succeeded in choosing two of almost every animal, a male and a female: a lion and a lioness; a cockroach and a cockraochess; a cock and a hen; a boy mouse and a girl mouse; a rabbit and a rabbitess; a man tortoise and a lady tortoise; a he-wolf and a she-wolf; a dog and a bitch; a crocodile and a crocodiless; a giraffe and a giraffess; a male and a female Baathist; and a queen ant and a king ant.

"I hope that the language know-it-alls won't interfere here regarding the rules of masculine and feminine, because I dream in slang."

As soon as I had boarded my ark, a great flood came and . . . then I woke up.

I had a cup of coffee and a cigarette while I watched the news in my room. I was surprised to see that the media was reporting on the closing ceremony of the convention of the International Association of the Masters of Arabic Poetry. One of the poets was reading the final statement and I listened to him, mesmerized.

What I gathered from the poet and then the presenter was that the conference had come up with some important recommendations to protect Arabic poetry. One of these recommendations emphasized the necessity of assassinating me, personally, due to the danger I posed to poetic meters and rhymes as well as to the prestige of the Arabic poem.

Unbothered, I switched off the TV and got dressed, intending to go to the market to do some shopping.

I left my room on the third floor. By the main door of the building, I spotted four poets who looked like they'd stepped out of the seventh century. They were driving a wooden trebuchet and were trying to park it between Haj Saleh's car and our neighbor Mahmoud's, next to the pavement. After a long struggle they finally succeeded; they jumped down from the trebuchet and came up to me.

"Good-e'en, fellow," they shouted in my face.

"Hi guys. Can I help you?"

One of them rushed back to the trebuchet and brought over a stone carving of a human face.

"Do you know this man?" he asked angrily, lifting it up with difficulty to show me. "Or where he lives?"

The carved face was similar to my own, but they didn't notice. I quickly realized that they had been sent by the conference of the International Association of the Masters of Arabic Poetry to assassinate me, in implementation of the conference recommendations. They had been selected from various poetic meters and rhymes so that my blood would be scattered and lost forever between different Arabic poems.

"What's this scumbag done to piss you off?"

"The bastard has mocked us for years," one of them snarled in my face like a lion. "He ridiculed the sacred poetry of the Arabic language in his writings during his drunken stupors. He's done this during ordinary as well as sacred months! He's written a story about us called *Help us Get Rid*

of Poets, and a play called *The Maid and the Family of Poets*. Damn him!
I swear by God I'll tear him apart."

He looked like someone who had been chewed upon by the vicissitudes
of aeons, their attacks, retreats, advancements, and regressions.

I liked this "tear apart"; it reminded me of cutting the bread for *fattoush*.
Trying hard to hide my laughter, I said, "The scumbag in your sculpture
lives here—third floor, door on the right."

"Thank you, Bedouin!" they yelled and hurried into the building, drawing daggers from their belts.

I laughed more heartily than I ever had before and walked off toward
the market.

My friend Kasem, the butcher, waved to me from the door of his shop. I
waved back; I liked Kasem a great deal. He was a master of separating meat
from the bone, empowering women, and keeping religion separate from
having fun while he was drinking.

"Why don't you slaughter a poet instead of a sheep?" I called to him
from a distance.

He laughed and asked, "Why do you want me to slaughter a poet?"

"Because I'm thinking of cooking poet *mulukhiyyah* tomorrow—a
mulukhiyyah that follows an archaic rhythm."

We laughed together. At that moment, Kasem's young son Yahya
grabbed his father's trousers.

"Dad!" he shouted. "Please will you buy us a colorful poet to raise on the
roof with the pigeons?"

We burst out laughing, some customers in the shop joining in. After a
while I went on my way.

As I neared the market, it felt like I was getting closer to the dark cave
of my life.

Trudging along the pavement I lit a cigarette and thought of a science
program I had watched a few days ago, where I had learned that, according

to scientists, life on this planet began three-and-a-half-billion years ago . . . But when would it end?

The market was unusually crowded, as if it was the day before Eid. The shops and pavements teemed with people. Then I glimpsed them amongst the crowds, some distance away. I gasped and rubbed my eyes, unable to believe what I was seeing. I moved closer to gaze at them between the passersby. It was my parents—yes, my mother and father who had died years ago. But they were not old as they had been when they died; they were as youthful as their pictures in the family album.

How beautiful my mother was as a young woman and how beautiful my father as a young man. How beautiful that time was. I lit another cigarette and old times flashed through my memory.

They didn't notice me as I got closer. I watched them intently, my heart hammering. I scrutinized their faces; it was impossible that they were anyone but my parents. Their voices also sounded the same.

They were carrying several bags and there was an excitable little boy jumping around them, seemingly tiring them out. They walked together through the crowded market with me following behind.

My mother stood on the pavement with the child and my father put his bags down beside them. They exchanged some words and then my father entered a fabric shop.

Next to me there was a cart selling vegetables. I started examining the produce so that my mother would not notice me as she waited for my father to come out of the shop. The child was jumping around like a devil when he suddenly fell from the curb and cried out in pain.

My mother threw down her bags and bent over him in fright. My heart pounded and I yearned for the old concern that had long ago lived in my mother's eyes.

A few passersby approached them. I rushed forward, squeezed myself through the small crowd and bent over the boy. His shoulder was cut, and my mother was hugging him anxiously. We looked at each other but she didn't recognize me.

I lifted the child from her lap onto the pavement and wiped the blood away with my handkerchief. Someone handed me a white clinical bandage which I wrapped deftly around the child's shoulder. Then my father came out, saw us, and gasped. He strode over and took the child out of my arms. Once reassured his son was OK, he and my mother turned and thanked me shyly, then they moved away, gently wiping their child's face.

Some mysterious force was stirring in me, and I followed them. When they entered the park, I walked in behind them and sat on the bench in front of theirs.

My father left while my mother stayed with the child on her lap. Her face was pale with worry. She tenderly wiped his face and started singing to him; a tear trickled down my cheek as my mother's old songs passed through my memory like a funeral procession.

My father came back with some corn on the cob he had bought from a vendor in the park. He gave one to the boy and watched with my mother as he devoured it.

My mom smiled widely, took another cob out of the bag and whispered something to the boy while my dad nodded.

The boy took the corn and walked over. He stopped in front of me and proffered it to me.

"This is for you, Uncle."

"Thank you."

"Thanks for helping me before."

I smiled at him and put the corncob aside. I re-tied the bandage around his shoulder as it had come loose.

"Don't tire your parents out too much," I told him. "They won't live with you forever."

"Yes, uncle."

"What's your name, you rascal?"

"Mustafa. What's yours?

I wanted to tell him that I was called Mustafa too, but the letters got caught in my throat and I couldn't pronounce my own name.

The boy waved to me happily and ran back to my parents. After a while they waved to me too, grateful for what I had done for their child, then picked up their bags and went home.

I stayed in the park, chain smoking and choking on my life.

When the sun set, I stood up wearily and walked off, dragging my feet. I meandered the streets slowly until I arrived home. Exhausted, I went up the stairs to the third floor. I opened the door of my room and switched on the light . . . then I gasped. My corpse was lying dumped on the floor, soaked in blood from several stab wounds.

I crouched down over my body and tenderly gathered it to my chest, weeping silently. Then I removed from it the remains of the torn shirt and gazed sorrowfully at the old scar on my shoulder.

I didn't care that I had been murdered; what I cared about was immortalizing this scar so that it would remain forever, even if just in a modest poem.

7th May, 2020
"Scar in a Modest Poem"
Taken from the Collection *Help us Get Rid of Poets*

Strange questions sometimes wandered around in my mind, questions for which I couldn't find any answers. Nor did I understand why my mind was so specialized in coming up with these questions.

Tonight, after a couple of glasses of wine in a tavern on the banks of the Bosphorus, I began to wonder to myself what was the relationship between the alleys of old Damascus and the attractive plump breasts of a beautiful woman? I was sure there must be a connection, but I didn't know what it was at that moment as I drank my wine, one glass after another.

It was after midnight when I left the tavern and staggered around wearily, dragging my feet. I realized that I had left some things behind on the table: my name and my lighter. I was very upset about the lighter, then I thought that I could buy another one, as well as a new name, from the nearest shop. I didn't go back to the tavern. I was quite convinced that I'd entered it nine years earlier but had only got out a few minutes ago.

I stood silently and watched as some laughing girls boarded a ship. I didn't know their nationalities, but I don't think the laughter of beautiful girls is specific to a language or nation.

The faraway echoes of their mirth sounded like ancient music that I'd heard before, but I couldn't remember where.

The ship set sail, slowly moving away. Where was it going with those girls on board, I wondered?

"Don't leave me alone here, ship!" I bellowed after it, feeling suddenly afraid.

But the ship didn't pay any attention to my shouting and carried on to disappear into the darkness of the night. It left me there on the banks of the Bosphorus, alone, on the cusp of turning forty; it bore away all the beautiful girls, took them back, far away, to my childhood.

"Hello there, mate," said a voice. "What are you looking at?"

A young man I didn't know stood next to me, looking at me in bewilderment. He offered me a cigarette that seemed to me like a bribe to make me answer him. I took it without looking at him.

"I'm watching a ship that was just here. It sailed off a little while ago to return to my childhood."

"Are you a poet?"

I turned to him angrily and replied, "Good God, no! Honestly, do I look like a poet? God forbid. I'm from a respectable family. I could've been an architect, but when the war started nine years ago, I had to flee. I came here and . . ."

"Are you drunk?"

"Yes, and without a lighter."

He staggered forward to light my cigarette.

"Come with me," he slurred, laughing. "If the poet police show up they might arrest us. It would be so shameful to be arrested for being a poet after so many years working as a dealer! And when I'm in prison, the cartels will be pointing and laughing, calling me a *poet!*"

Frankly, I was afraid; anything was better than the accusation of being a poet. We walked away from the water, leaning on each other a little.

I tried to remember a song, any sweet song I loved, but I couldn't. They always deserted me when I really needed them.

"I drink behind that wooden cart where you buy grilled fish. It's my cart and I sleep behind it every night."

I inclined my head as he pointed at his cart then we sat down behind it on a small rug. He smiled at me and turned around to open a drawer under the cart, taking from it a bottle of wine and two glasses.

"To your health!" he shouted, passing me a glass.

"To your health," I echoed.

We drank together, talked, and laughed. Neither of us asked the other his name. I think the wine we were drinking and the ship that had returned to the place we also wished to go had made us forget everything.

"What do you do for a living these days?" he asked me after a while.

"Hmmm . . . I can't remember. Every night I forget the personality I had during the day, then during the day I forget the one I had at night."

He was in the process of pouring a fresh glass of wine but paused, as if afraid of giving a glass to an enemy.

"Are you a poet?"

"Good God, no! Honestly, do I look like a poet? I'm from a respectable family. I could've been a textile merchant like my father, but the war that started nine years ago brought me here and . . ."

He handed me the glass.

"To your health!" I shouted, full of confidence.

"To your health!"

"Where are you from?" he asked. He was looking at a spot beside me, but I was sure the question was meant for me.

"I don't remember exactly, but I'm sure that in 1857 I was in a city called Damascus. What year are we in now?"

He thought for a while as he lit a cigarette.

"I don't know," he said, looking confused. "Why are your questions so difficult?"

Shortly after, a young homeless woman passed by in front of the cart and noticed us. She sat down, smiling at us. She looked at us and saw in my eyes a ship returning to her childhood. She turned away so as not to cry. She stared at my friend and understood that he was the owner of this corner, the bottle of wine, the cigarettes, and the lighter.

The woman winked at my friend and offered to flash us for a glass of wine and a cigarette. We laughed together: she, he, and I and the remains of a city in my head. He poured her a glass and passed her a lit cigarette.

We drank several glasses together, smoked, laughed, and sang songs that we couldn't fully recollect. From afar the sound of the ships played incomplete pieces of music for us.

The young woman drank and smoked, sometimes looking at the sea with hidden sadness.

"I missed the ship that just left for your childhood," she whispered drunkenly to me, close to tears.

Every woman is both an angel and a whore, a mysterious and contradictory blend of warmth and coldness—a paradox. But for a creature like me, who forgets his lighter and even his name in taverns, it's hard to tell when she is one or the other. The line between the two is so thin, it's nearly invisible to the drunk.

She put another cigarette between her lips and looked at us mischievously while taking hold of the hem of her shirt. She paused, watching our eyes which were shining and ready, and then, just like the theater curtain going up at the beginning of a play I attended in Damascus in 1857, the girl lifted her shirt right up, laughing and covering her face bashfully.

We looked at her breasts and I remembered a city that I had fled a thousand years ago. The girl lowered her shirt, laughing. I lit another cigarette and offered it to her, leaning on the ground as if prostrating myself in a prayer that I had last uttered twenty years before.

"A cigarette for this infinite whiteness," I whispered.

Annoyed, she took it from me.

"Are you a poet?" she asked angrily.

"Good God, no! Honestly, do I look like a poet? I'm from a respectable family. I could've been a tailor in my mother's shop, but the war that began nine years ago is . . ."

She remembered her mother, I remembered my mother, the young man who owned the fish cart remembered his. None of them were still with us; they were all now in the other world.

I don't remember when the girl left, nor falling asleep. I awoke suddenly in the early morning; the young owner of the cart was arranging the fish that had arrived a short while ago and people were passing by here and there.

I got up and started to walk away.

"Look over there!" the young man called from behind me. "That ship that went to your childhood last night came back a little while ago."

I turned to him and shouted angrily, "Are you a poet?"

He put his finger to his lips, signaling to me to shut up. He looked around to make sure that no one had heard my accusation, fearing for his reputation and the potential decline in sales of his fish.

"Good God, no!" he said confidently. "I'm from a respectable family, and I own the cart that sells the best grilled fish on the banks of the Bosphorus."

I smiled at him and walked off. I hailed a taxi to take me to my room, where I had a shower and drank a strong cup of coffee.

I got dressed and went out to work, and it was like I was a different creature.

On the way, I tried to remember the person I'd been the night before but I simply couldn't.

"Where were you last night?" my colleague asked me. "I tried calling you a few times and you didn't answer."

"I was in Damascus," I answered, not looking at him. "I saw the two most beautiful neighborhoods in the world."

"Asshole! Are you a poet?"

"Good God, no! I'm from a respectable family."

9th November, 2019
"Remains of Strangers on the Banks of the Bosphorus"
Taken from the collection *Help us Get Rid of Poets*

Every Syrian who fled their country during the war has their own story, and their own fantasies too, and I am one of them. Due to the magnitude of the tragedy, I can no longer distinguish between fiction and reality.

But before you read my story, dear reader, I would like to ask you: are you a believer? You will answer *yes*, and so I hope you do not die to save me, the infidel.

Three believers save a non-believer

For years, my friends have unfortunately accused me of being a non-believer. These accusations, I believe, are untrue. I am not good at practicing religious rituals because I grew up in a religiously neutral environment. As a result, I did not learn them, and that is basically it.

I do not have the convictions of an atheist, but nor do I have the behaviors or habits of a believer. Believers in sorrow are very similar to atheists in sorrow.

In sorrow, you cannot tell one from the other.

Thus, I have lived my life as though I am a flute that does not realize it is a flute. Sometimes it is believers who pick up the flute to play their sorrows, and at other times it is non-believers.

I am a flute that failed to save his mother, as it is apparently the wont of flutes to do.

They were all sad. The whole city was sad and exhausted by the war. I escaped that city in April 2014 with the help of three believers from different religions and sects. I did not know them very well, nor did they know one another. They had been my father's acquaintances before he passed away in 2012. I asked them for help to survive.

Jaber, from Tartus, was involved in Air Force Intelligence and a member of the Alawite sect. His job meant he used to frequent the government institution where my mother worked almost daily. While roaming the employees' offices, Jaber would stick his head around the door of my mother's office to say hello, then go on his way. Jaber loved my father dearly even though my father—a communist dissident writer since the 1980s—did not like security personnel. Nevertheless, he and Jaber struck up a friendship after several encounters that attested to his integrity and love of helping others. Jaber's house was close to ours. My mother and Jaber's wife regularly exchanged visits over the years.

One day he entered my mother's office in a hurry. This was not his habit. He closed the door behind him, moved close to her and whispered a warning: "Tell your son to get out of town immediately. Advise him to go to the countryside. I've received information that his name is going to be circulated among the checkpoints. He must leave tomorrow morning."

He hurried out of my mother's office, looking as though a heavy weight had been lifted. My mother rushed home from work early. She told me what she had heard, then called Jaber and handed me her mobile. He spoke to me as though he were trying to avoid being understood by anyone else. "Go to your grandfather's house in the village, and don't worry—God is with us."

I felt as if his hand was holding my shoulder unseen, shaking me encouragingly as he reiterated, "Don't worry—God is with us and He will deliver us."

An hour and a half later, my mother had packed a suitcase for me. We did not intend for me to stay home that night; instead, we called a friend of my father, a Christian engineer whose office was located in the town center, where I would be able to hide until morning.

I stood in my room to take a farewell look at the library: more than 7,000 books collected by my late father, volume by volume, before I was born. The library and I had grown up together.

I headed to the engineering office, taking the subway far away from the checkpoints. I sat down with the engineer and we chatted and reminisced about my father. The man decided to go home after I told him I would have to leave in the morning, before he arrived for work, and would not be coming back due to my critical situation. He grabbed my shoulder and shook me, smiling confidently, and repeating, "Don't worry—God is with us and He will deliver us."

That night I could not sleep. I had been put in touch with a Sunni sheikh who presided over an armed faction of the opposition on the outskirts of the city. He too was one of my father's acquaintances; my mother, who knew his aunt, had spoken to him. Later on he phoned me, explaining that the town was completely controlled by security members and military forces, while opposition factions were besieging it from all directions. That situation went on for more than three years, from 2012 to 2015.

He told me they had a car that came to Idlib every morning in collusion with the army and security checkpoints. This car patrolled the streets of the city for a few hours, collecting food, medicine, and other things for the armed men, before driving back out to them. He explained that I would get out of town in this car. The car was so special that security and military personnel stationed at the checkpoints would never check my ID. I felt reassured and gave him the go-ahead, along with my address. Then I roamed around the office and flicked through some books, talked to myself a lot, and smoked heavily; it was my last night in Idlib.

The car arrived at my address in the morning. I left the office and got in with my suitcase. The car was full of sacks. The man drove off and I sat behind him, feeling very nervous. I bade farewell to Idlib, road by road.

Looking at the crowded marketplace through the window, I bade farewell to the faces of people walking there. None of them noticed me, and so none of them said goodbye.

I could hardly believe it when we passed the last and largest of the security and military checkpoints. We were not inspected by anyone. Nobody requested our ID cards. A soldier took an envelope containing a sum of money from the driver and motioned to us to pass through quickly.

A hundred meters beyond the checkpoint, the driver laughed, looked at me in the rear-view mirror and said, "We're in the liberated territories." I breathed a deep sigh of relief.

A quarter of an hour later we arrived at a farm. A group of young men with guns slung over their shoulders hurried to meet us. I got out of the car by the front door. One of the men asked me to enter, and there was the sheikh waiting for me inside, surrounded by many armed men. He welcomed me and we went and sat by the swimming pool to drink tea and smoke together. I quickly realized that the sheikh had a great deal of information about me: my studies at the School of Media, my articles published in newspapers and on social media, my deceased father, the books he wrote, and his long-standing problems with the regime.

"Would you like to work with us?" he asked. "There's a house behind the farm; it's yours if you want it. We can give you photos of the battles as well as other videos and information, you could use them to write and publish articles that reach the people. We have the internet and modern equipment; we'll help you and provide you with everything you need."

"I want to go to Turkey," I whispered to him. "I feel suffocated in this country. I'll return to you when my circumstances get better."

He gripped my shoulder and shook me as I looked carefully at the features of his kind face. He whispered to me, "Don't worry—God is with us and He will deliver us."

He reminded me of one of those popular folk heroes you read about in novels who rise up from among the people, with humble education and high conscience, and, with unintentional little mistakes, lead the people in good faith.

I slept that night at the farm where the sheikh lived and from which he managed his battles and dozens of his own soldiers, along with other factions next to his own.

The next morning the sheikh summoned a car and instructed one of his soldiers to take me to the Turkish border. The car moved along and we passed through the villages in the countryside north of Idlib. After about an hour and a half we reached the Orontes River. There were many people crossing to the other bank, the Turkish side. For a hefty amount of money, I managed to reserve a space in a 'pot': a small boat that could accommodate up to ten passengers, taking them to the opposite bank within minutes. When I arrived on the other side, I did not feel that I was in Turkey, a different country; it was as if the borders were nothing but lies.

I got on a minibus with the others that drove us to Reyhanli, a Turkish border town by the river. I got off in the town square. I asked a few people about accommodation, and they directed me to a nearby hotel. I headed there and booked a room for three days. Then I phoned my mother to reassure her that I had arrived safely. My life in Turkey began on the 20th of April 2014.

During my first days there, I contacted all the people I knew who had preceded me in escaping here. I met up with some of them, and one showed me another hotel where I could settle permanently; this hotel was next to Lake Yenişehir, in an area allocated for Turkish students, and charged a modest rent.

In the months that followed my escape the three men were killed, one after another. The Alawite security agent was killed in an ambush inside the town. The Christian engineer was killed by a stray shell that hit the town marketplace one day. The Sunni sheikh died with his wife after someone laced their food with poison; the operation was allegedly labelled an internal liquidation within his faction.

The three believers who saved a non-believer were not saved by God. God did not help them but did help me, the non-believer. This thought would haunt me in the years following their deaths and my escape from Idlib.

My days in Reyhanli

My room was on the second floor of the Miray Otel. In front of the building there was a large, lovely park set up by the municipality around the beautiful lake. Some modest cafés and pubs were scattered around the lakeside. I met an old Turkish man who ran a simple pub overlooking the water opposite the hotel, and began to visit his place from time to time. The old man and I quickly became friends; he spoke Arabic modestly well. I began frequenting his pub every evening. His customers were very few. They could be counted on the fingers of one hand. He would pour them glasses of wine and prepare simple dishes. A song resounded from an old machine in the corner; a beautiful but sad Turkish song. I did not understand the lyrics, but the old man played it several times a night to the point that I learned the words by heart, still without understanding their meaning.

During my university days in Damascus I had not been much of a drinker, probably once a week or fortnight and on special occasions. But after arriving in Reyhanli I rapidly became an alcoholic in this old man's pub.

The first year and the start of the second went by slowly and were terribly boring. The factions took control of Idlib in March 2015. I could not go back as some did for fear of the extremists. I tried my best to bring my mother to Reyhanli to save her from Idlib's hell, but I failed.

The idea occurred to me to re-read Dostoevsky's novels. I missed those novels, which I had read as a preparatory school student some 20 years earlier. I called my mother at home and asked her to find the books in our big library. After asking many friends in Reyhanli I managed to contact a man who was able to travel across the border from Idlib daily, since he had a businessman's card. His name was Mahmoud and his features were very rough and crude.

I understood from friends that he brought heavy loads from Idlib for acquaintances in exchange for a fee. I phoned this man and met him at the park by the lake. He looked at photos of the books my mother had sought out for me on my mobile phone, pursed his lips and said, "I can't bring all the books in one go. I have lots of orders already. I could bring you a book a week; what do you think?"

I agreed and gave him the amount he requested. He would in fact charge less for future deliveries of Dostoevsky's novels, because as soon as he arrived at our home to get the first one, my mother realized that Mahmoud, whom I had told her about over the phone, was a former employee of the government institution where she worked.

The Idiot

Toward the end of September 2015 Mahmoud arrived from Idlib. He called me and we met by the lake. I saw them by his side, carrying bundles of clothes on their shoulders like anyone hastily displaced and escaping the war: Myshkin, Nastasya, Parfyon and Gavril—the heroes of Dostoevsky's *The Idiot*.

Mahmoud gave me the novel and told me briefly and resentfully about the painstaking task of smuggling it here. He spoke about his fear that extremists at the checkpoints in Idlib and its surrounding countryside might suspect him, and the problems that could be encountered if they saw this book with him.

I gave him the money and thanked him. We left him behind and walked away toward my room, Myshkin, Nastasya, Parfyon, Gavril and me.

They wandered around my room for a long time as I browsed the pages of this old edition, which my father had bought in the mid '80s when it was published by the Soviet company Raduga Publishers.

The days passed painfully slowly. I woke up late and read *The Idiot* until evening, then left my room at Miray Otel to walk around the lake a little and watch people silently. I walked by the lake, looking at the water; the song from the old Turkish pub would resound in my head and I did not know what it meant.

Around sunset, I would head toward the old man's pub to drink until late.

When I left, drunk, after midnight they were standing gathered at the door. They had set an airtight ambush for me, Myshkin, Nastasya, Parfyon and Gavril.

I gazed at them silently. They gazed back malevolently. They whispered to me with voices full of unnatural hatred, echoing as one: "Three believers, each in their own way, died to save this infidel."

Terrified and staggering, I hurried back to my room. Exhausted, I got into bed, tucked myself under the covers, and crammed my head under the pillow.

The four of them lifted my bed by the corners and spun it around in the middle of the room in the darkness, screaming throughout my restless sleep, "Three believers were killed to save this infidel."

The Adolescent

In mid-October, Mahmoud called and arranged to meet me in an hour's time, near the lake. I coldly shook hands with him. On his right, I saw Arkady, Versilov, and Lisa. I gave him the money and walked back to my room with them: the heroes of *The Adolescent*. They carried their bundles of clothes on their shoulders. They sighed in great relief at having escaped Idlib safely, at miraculously surviving the missiles.

I finished *The Adolescent* within days. On the last day of reading, I went to the pub late and drank with the old man. He helped me get up and prepared to close the pub. I walked to the door with difficulty—and there they were together, waiting for me, Arkady, Versilov and Lisa. They repeated in pale, gravelly voices, "Three believers were killed to save this infidel."

I hurried drunk to my room, stumbling over my own feet. I threw my body onto the bed with unbearable fatigue while the protagonists of *The Adolescent* revolved around me in a painful delirium. They screamed on and on in the darkness of my room as I lay half asleep: "Three believers were killed to save this infidel."

The Brothers Karamazov

Mahmoud gave me *The Brothers Karamazov* by the lake during the first week of November. I helped Father Fyodor to carry his bundle, which was huge and heavy, and we walked silently—me, Father Fyodor, Dmitri, Ivan, Ilyusha, Smerdyakov, the Jezebel Grushenka and the Elder Father Zosima.

They told me in anguished words and overwhelming distress about the horrible shelling of Idlib. They described how our house had survived bombardment by chance several times, how books, shelves, windows, and doors had all tumbled down, and how my mother had had to keep tidying up the house as best she could.

I started reading *The Brothers Karamazov* at the onset of winter; this novel which, itself, resembled an endless winter.

But on rainy nights, whenever I walked out of the pub after midnight, Father Fyodor, Dmitri, Ivan, Ilyusha, Smerdyakov, the Jezebel Grushenka, and the Elder Father Zosima chased me madly to my room, as if they had some revenge to exact upon me.

Sometimes they would revolve around my bed in a horrible nocturnal mystic ritual that would ravage my emotions and increase my pain. At other times, they would lift up the bed as I lay on it, half asleep and half dead, and start spinning it relentlessly and tirelessly as though it were my coffin, besieging me with nightmares as they shrieked in dry, monotonous voices, in a way that caused pain to every cell in my body: "Three believers were killed to save this infidel."

Crime and Punishment

Raskolnikov, Sonya, Razumikhin, and Porfiry were right behind Mahmoud, carrying bundles of clothes on their shoulders. In mid-December, Mahmoud stood between us to give me *Crime and Punishment* and pass on my mother's greetings. I said goodbye to Mahmoud and took the new Dostoevskian characters displaced from Idlib to my room in order to start reading.

In the pub the old owner said to me, "Hey, you've been visiting my pub for nearly two years, my friend, but you've never brought a friend. Don't you have any? Reyhanli is full of Syrians!"

Shyly, I explained to him that I had been an anti-social person since childhood, and had not had any friends throughout my life, either before or after the war, other than the fictional characters in the novels. I do not know if he understood my words well, but he poured a drink for himself and sat at my table to drink with me until late into the night.

Before I left, he told me with a misery that suited his old age, "Drunks have no friends but the bottle."

I staggered as I walked to the door, assuming that there would be a newly laid ambush waiting there for me.

From the door of the pub to the door of my room, my head, heavy with drink, felt ready to explode in the rain amid the screams of Raskolnikov,

Sonya, Razumikhin, and Porfiry, which sounded like the howls of wounded wolves.

To these wounded wolves my crime was the killing of the Alawite security member, the Christian engineer, and the Sunni sheikh; this rainy night was the courtroom and Dostoevsky's heroes were my punishment.

Their noise was incessant throughout that sleepless and exhausting night as they wailed grotesquely over my bed: "Three believers were killed because of this infidel."

Demons and The Gambler

By the end of 2015 I had become a gambler who had placed a bet on his soul when he smuggled all of Dostoevsky's demons out of Idlib. He had intended to fight the boredom of displacement from the place of his childhood. But these demons were fighting the gambler due to a crime that had brought together three believers from different religions and sects. They did not know one another but had all been killed during the war. They had never met in real life but did so all the time in my head.

On New Year's Eve, Mahmoud brought me *Demons* and *The Gambler*. He reported that my mother had told him Dostoevsky's books were done with. These were all of his works in our home library. I thanked him. He left bewildered, as was always the case whenever I met him to receive a novel. He was disquieted by my lost look, as if I could see something he could not.

Alexis and Polina from *The Gambler*, Stepan, Varvara, and Nikolai from *Demons* had with them small bundles of clothes when they arrived from Idlib. As usual, I led them silently to my room. During the first weeks of 2016, I finished reading *The Gambler* and *Demons*. I did not change my evening habits of walking around the lake, examining the humans closely, even when it was raining, and frequenting the old Turkish man's pub.

Likewise, the disturbing ambushes set for me whenever I got drunk, and the nightmares caused by the fictional characters also continued.

I left the pub at midnight and saw them together: Alexis, Polina, Stepan, Varvara, and Nikolai. Their faces took on strange, brutal shapes behind me as they savagely repeated from the pub to my bed, "Three believers died because of this infidel."

Face to face with Dostoevsky's wolves on a rainy winter's night

I made a mistake when I smuggled Dostoevsky's heroes from Idlib to Reyhanli. They had become an unbearable, agonizing nightmare for me. They had turned into disturbing creatures accusing me of a crime I did not commit. Regardless of their beliefs, it was those believers' destiny that had committed the crime against them. I had nothing to do with it.

That night I came back drunk to my room. As soon as I entered, they surrounded my body with their own bodies, from all sides. Resentment and hatred were dripping from their faces, as if they were black clouds that showered me with dark rain, as if they were taking revenge on me for those believers who had been killed after they saved me.

Myshkin, Nastasya, Parfyon, and Gavril; Arkady, Versilov and Lisa; Father Fyodor, Dmitri, Ivan, Ilyusha, Smerdyakov, the Jezebel Grushenka, and the Elder Father Zosima; Raskolnikov, Sonya, Razumikhin, and Porfiry; Alexis and Polina; Stepan, Varvara, and Nikolai: all the members of the Dostoevskian tribe were ruthlessly repeating in front of me, "Three believers were killed after they saved an infidel."

"You bastards, I saved you and brought you here from Idlib!" I yelled. "Damn you. Why are you causing me so much pain?"

Nobody responded. The despicable Raskolnikov interrupted them, gesturing with a hand for them to shut up, and they fell silent. He headed to my table and began browsing through some photos I had brought with me when I left Idlib, memories of the various stages of my life:

childhood, adolescence, and university years, in Idlib, Damascus, Homs, Hama, Latakia, and Lebanon.

It seemed by his facial expression that my photos scattered on the table disturbed him, as he examined them one by one.

Suddenly he turned and shouted at me like an interrogator, "Are these your photos?"

"Yes, they're mine; I've had them since I was a child. Is there something wrong with them?"

He rubbed his chin, confused, then smiled at me maliciously. It seemed he had found in my photos the evidence to condemn me for any crime in the universe. He muttered with disturbing calmness, "Dozens of photos of only you, over so many years. They're all of you, alone! You don't have a single photo with friends or even one friend, with relatives, with family, or with anyone at all."

"It wasn't something I paid attention to."

Raskolnikov approached me, contemplating my face as a blood-red hue crept into his eyes. Waving some of my photos in front of me and in front of the eyes of Dostoevsky's heroes, he whispered to me with confidence, "Do you realize that whoever takes the time to browse your photos will be made certain that you're a criminal, and that you are the one who committed those crimes against those three believers? You have no friends whatsoever, that's natural. The crime has no friends, even before it's committed." He giggled as he repeated, "The crime has no friends, even before it's committed."

I snatched a bottle of wine off my table. Exhausted, I raised it to my mouth to drink what was left, and they all chanted together, like members of a choir for the dead in the afterworld, "Three believers were killed because of this infidel."

I ran away from them. I left my room on that rainy night before they could suffocate me. I could no longer tolerate them and their madness. My life was not a novel in which they could do whatever pleased them and appeased their dark fury.

I returned to the pub. The old owner was still there, sitting alone. I sat next to him, looking through the window at the characters of Dostoevsky's novels scattered along the street from the door of the pub to the lake, in the moonlight and the rain, as if they were on a night-time demonstration against me, shouting loudly: "Three believers were killed because of this infidel!"

The old man was not surprised by my return. Over the years, he had become accustomed to the weird behavior of drunks. He brought me a drink and I lit two cigarettes, one for him and one for me.

I drank a lot; I kept drinking till dawn. The old man slumbered in his chair. I left the pub dragging my feet.

Dostoevsky's heroes were lying on the ground, surrendered to sleep. I was tired. I walked to the lake and sat down next to it. I contemplated the water, which stretched on to the horizon. When I looked at the water, my soul was calmed a little bit.

Soon after, a young man whom I did not know sat beside me and asked, "Where are you from, brother?"

"I don't know, I've forgotten."

He was surprised by my words. Without turning to him I carelessly asked, "Where are you from?"

The sun was shining shyly on this winter morning as he replied, "Idlib."

I took a deep drag on my cigarette. He looked at me, bewildered. Still without facing him I asked, "Are you a believer?"

"Of course," he responded, so I whispered, "Then beware! You might die because of me, the infidel."

I do not think he had ever had a more mysterious morning than this one in his entire life. The remnants of alcohol in my head prompted me to whisper to this stranger, "You know something, I managed to smuggle

Dostoevsky's heroes out of Idlib, but I couldn't get my mother out! It seems that mercy knows its way to fictional heroes but not how to reach the people of Idlib."

I fell silent for a while to take a drag on my cigarette, then added with something like certainty, "If the people of Idlib were fictional characters, they would have escaped and survived this war."

He did not understand anything I was saying. I got up wearily and walked back to my room.

They woke up one by one, Dostoevsky's heroes. They followed behind me, as if we were walking in a funeral procession. The sun rose above us as we approached my room and they whispered loudly and repeatedly together behind me, "Three believers were killed to save this infidel. Three believers were killed to save this infidel. Three believers were killed to save this infidel."

I started singing that Turkish song in time to my footsteps; the song from the pub whose meaning I still did not know. I sang it to this life whose meaning I could not understand either.

What if this war ends, and one day I return to Idlib? What will I do?

I will sing this song for those who are still alive, who have somehow managed to survive the war, this song that I do not understand. We will dance happily, raucously, and madly; we will dance to its melodies, without understanding its meaning.

Istanbul, 12th March, 2019
"Smuggling Dostoevsky's Heroes Out of Idlib"
Taken from the Collection *Help us Get Rid of Poets*

www.ingramcontent.com/pod-product-compliance
Lightning Source LLC
Chambersburg PA
CBHW032031270525
27155CB00016B/144